JASMINE
ROTTMAN

star power

Blast from the Past

Catch Star's act!

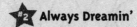
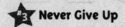
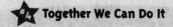
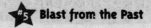
A new book drops every other month!
Next up:

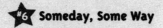
From Aladdin Paperbacks
Published by Simon & Schuster

#5

star power

Blast from the Past

by Catherine Hapka

Aladdin Paperbacks
New York   London   Toronto   Sydney

First Aladdin Paperbacks edition November 2004

Copyright © 2004 by Catherine Hapka

ALADDIN PAPERBACKS
An imprint of Simon & Schuster
Children's Publishing Division
1230 Avenue of the Americas
New York, NY 10020

Designed by Debra Sfetsios
The text of this book was set in Triplex.
Printed in the United States of America
2 4 6 8 10 9 7 5 3 1

Library of Congress Control Number 2003116538
ISBN 0-689-86791-3

#5

star power

Blast from the Past

One

Star Calloway's feet pounded on the ground beneath her. Her breath came in short gasps, and sweat poured down her face and back as she ran. The muscles in her legs ached from exertion. She glanced over her shoulder at the stocky, swarthy man behind her.

"Don't slow down!" he barked. "Keep moving!"

"Aargh!" Star cried, certain that she couldn't go on any longer.

She reached forward and turned a lever on the panel directly in front of her. Immediately the moving rubber grid beneath her slowed down, allowing her to break to a brisk walk.

When she got her breath back, she glanced over at the man. "Tank, if I didn't know better, I'd think you didn't like me or something."

Star's bodyguard and personal trainer, Tank Massimo, only grinned in response. Stepping toward the treadmill, he turned the lever up again. The movement caused the muscles in his arms to ripple impressively.

"Three more minutes," he ordered. "Then you can hit the shower."

Breaking back into a jog, Star groaned loudly. "If I survive that long," she grumbled.

"You'd better," Tank said calmly. "You've got another concert tomorrow night."

Despite her tired muscles, Star felt a little flutter of excitement at that. Sometimes it was hard for her to believe that she was really on her first worldwide concert tour. Of course, it was still a little hard to believe that she was an international singing superstar at the age of fourteen. The past two years of her life had been like an incredible dream—in most ways, anyway.

Star glanced around at the spacious room full of gleaming, high-tech exercise equipment. The gym in this particular hotel was located on the very top floor of the high-rise building, and huge picture windows on three sides of the room showed off a spectacular view of the German cityscape below. As Star's gaze wandered past the leather-padded doors leading out to the elevator bank, she noticed a group of her backup dancers clustered around a row of vending machines, gulping down bottled water.

"Hey," Star said to Tank, who was leaning on a nearby weight bench. "How come you're not making *them* do three more minutes?"

One of the dancers, a pretty strawberry blond in her late teens named Rachel Maxwell, heard her. "He already ran us ragged, remember?" she called to Star. "While you were stretching, Tank was making us do all kinds of evil push-ups and lunges and stuff."

"That's right," Rachel's twin sister, Erin, called out. "We'll be lucky if we're not too sore to dance tomorrow."

Tank rolled his eyes as all the dancers giggled. "If you're too sore, it won't be because of that," he said. "It'll be because things've been so busy lately you haven't spent enough time in the gym." He added a few grumbled words under his breath in a foreign language Star didn't recognize.

She grinned. Tank spoke at least seventeen foreign languages, which made it hard to understand his words sometimes. Fortunately his kind brown eyes were always easy to read, and Star could see that he wasn't really upset.

"You know we're only teasing you, Tank," she said breathlessly.

Tank's eyes twinkled. "I know, Star-baby," he assured her. "And I know you've been working hard on this tour—

especially this past week. I don't know what Mike was think-ing, scheduling five concerts in six days."

"He said it was the only way he could work it out so we could cover those particular two cities in Germany," Star said, recalling a conversation that morning with her man-ager, Mike Mosley. "He was mega worried about it too, but he figured we could handle it. That's why this break coming up is nice and long. He wanted to give all of us plenty of time to rest before we get back to work."

As much as Star loved being on tour, she was looking for-ward to flying home to New Limpet, Pennsylvania. It would be a nice, long visit during the two-week break coming up after their next stop in Switzerland. Her grandmother's birth-day fell during that time, and Star had already made plans to throw a huge celebration for her.

"That's three," Tank said, breaking into her thoughts. "Star? You can stop now. Unless you want me to set you up for another fifteen minutes, of course . . ."

"No!" Star said quickly, slowing down to a walk and then finally coming to a stop. She leaned over to rest her hands on her knees. Now that she wasn't moving, a whole new wave of exhaustion swept over her. "That's okay. I was just a little distracted there for a sec."

Tank chuckled and switched off the machine. "Thinking about ways to get back at me for those extra three minutes?"

"Of course!" Star grinned, glancing up at him. She straightened to a standing position, groaning slightly with the effort, then reached up to adjust her curly blonde pony-tail. "No, actually I was thinking about Nans. I can't wait to see her—I've never been apart from her for so long, at least not since . . ."

She let her voice trail off. Tank was already nodding under-standingly. Star's parents and baby brother had disappeared during a boat trip in Florida almost two years earlier. The police still had no idea what had happened to them, but Star had never given up hope that they would find some answers if she was patient.

She touched the silver star necklace hanging over the neckline of her sports top. A cherished gift from her parents that she never took off, the necklace was her way of keeping her family with her in spirit while they couldn't be there in person. For a second, a wave of homesickness almost over-whelmed her—not only for her grandmother and her home-town friends, but for her missing family as well.

Then she looked over at Tank, who was gazing at her with concern. She forced the lonely feelings down, reminding herself that she was still one of the luckiest girls in the world. Whenever her parents finally returned, she was certain they would tell her the exact same thing.

"Come on," she told Tank, stifling a yawn as her weariness threatened to overtake her. "Let's get out of here."

Star and Tank said good-bye to the backup dancers and headed for the elevators. As Tank punched the button, Star could hear the dancers making plans to grab a bite to eat at the hotel coffee shop. Even though she knew she would be welcome to join them if she wanted to, Star couldn't help feeling a little left out. She was starting to become pretty good friends with several of the dancers, especially Rachel and Erin, but she still felt a little weird about hanging out with them sometimes. She was only fourteen, whereas the youngest dancers were at least four years older. Even though the tour had her name on it, spending so much time with older people sometimes made Star feel like a little kid at a grown-up party, trying not to do anything immature that would have her sent off to bed early and make her miss all the fun.

But she shook off the feeling, knowing she was being silly. Besides, at the moment her thoughts were still focused on the upcoming trip home.

"I can't wait to see what Nans thinks of the gifts I got her for her birthday," she told Tank. "I also can't wait to see who turns up at her party this year."

"What do you mean?" Tank asked.

The elevator doors slid open. Star stepped inside, followed by the bodyguard.

"Well, let's just say it's sort of a tradition," Star told Tank with a grin. "Nans just can't resist inviting anyone and everyone she meets to her parties, especially if she thinks they look lonely. Like, a couple of years ago she just had to drag home the lovely young man she met at a bus stop. Boy, was he confused! Especially since he'd just flown in from Korea and barely spoke English . . ."

Tank chuckled. "Sounds like your grandmother to me," he said. "The first time I met her, she insisted she'd just knitted a sweater that would look wonderful on me."

"I remember that." Star stifled another yawn, leaning against the elevator wall, even though she knew it would probably leave a smudge mark on the polished brass. Just about everything in the hotel seemed to be made of polished brass. "You wore that sweater just a few nights ago when it got so chilly."

"Of course," Tank replied. "It's my favorite."

"Anyway, that bus stop guy wasn't the only one," Star went on as the elevator doors slid open on their floor. "There was the year she invited the meter reader, and then the next year she brought home a salesgirl from the mall. And of course there's almost always someone new from her beauty shop— she goes there every week, so she's always meeting the new shampooist or the girl they've just hired to sweep up hair."

Tank led the way down the quiet, elegantly decorated hotel hallway. "That must keep things interesting," he said.

"It does." Star shrugged. "I guess to Nans, the whole world is just full of best friends she hasn't met yet."

Tank winked at her. "Reminds me of someone else I know," he said as they reached the door to their suite. "Someone about four feet eleven, with curly blonde hair . . ."

Star glanced at her own petite, curly-blonde-haired reflection in the gleaming brass key plate on the suite door. She smiled, knowing that Tank was right—like her grandmother, she preferred to think of every stranger as a friend in the making. It made the world seem a lot friendlier.

When they opened the door to the suite, the main room was bustling with activity. The first thing Star saw was her dog, a chubby fawn pug named Dudley Do-Wrong, leaping forward to greet her. She bent to hug him, then straightened up and looked around. Boxes, trunks, and suitcases were scattered everywhere. Star's full-time tutor, a handsome sixtysomething woman named Mrs. Magdalene Nattle, was standing at the counter of the suite's alcove kitchenette. Mags, as most of Star's team called her, glanced up and gave Star and Tank a quick wave before returning to her task of packing soda bottles and packages of food into a large plastic cooler, her hands moving so fast it made Star feel more tired than ever.

In the center of the luxurious main room Star spotted Lola LaRue, a pleasantly plump African-American woman dressed in fuchsia stretch pants and zebra-print stilettos. Lola, who served as Star's stylist and head wardrobe person, was sorting through a cardboard box perched on the arm of a beige upholstered chair. Nearby, bits and pieces of Star's stage costumes were draped all over the suite's fancy furniture, while bottles of shampoo, hair dryers, tubes of makeup, and other paraphernalia were scattered across the tasteful Oriental rug.

Meanwhile a tall, mustached man wearing purple cowboy boots was standing beneath the brass-and-crystal chandelier in the open foyer, holding a cell phone in one hand and a clipboard in the other. A half-packed box of publicity materials sat open at his feet.

He glanced up when Star and Tank stepped into the room with Dudley winding his way around their ankles. "There y'all are," he greeted them in a deep Texas drawl, sounding frazzled. "Was just about to send out a search party. 'Cept we couldn't spare anybody to go, not if we want to get this mess packed up in time to leave for Switzerland tomorrow morning."

"We're ready to pitch in, Mike," Star promised, doing her best to force down her own weariness. "Just let me hop in the shower, and I'll be ready to go."

She hurried off toward one of the suite's bathrooms. Within minutes she was feeling not only cleaner, but also slightly more awake, thanks to the super-powered water jets in the large glassed-in shower stall. Unfortunately the feeling didn't last long, and by the time she finished toweling off her blonde hair and left the room, she was yawning again. She couldn't help glancing wistfully into her bedroom as she walked past, though she ignored the craving to go in and flop down on the comfortable bed. There was work to be done, and she wanted to do her part.

"I'm back," she announced as she reentered the main room. She smiled sleepily at Mike, who was still holding his cell phone and clipboard as he watched Tank add a box to the top of the growing pile near the door. "What do you want me to—"

Her words were interrupted by the shrill tone of Mike's cell phone. He punched a button and put it to his ear.

"Mosley here," he said. As he listened, one eyebrow shot up in surprise. "Mr. Lukas!" he exclaimed. "Thanks for getting back to me so quickly. So how's things?"

Star and Tank exchanged a glance. They had met Lukas Lukas, the well-known Swedish film director, during a recent tour stop in his home country. The eccentric auteur had agreed to direct the video for Star's next single, "Blast from the Past." Star had spent a few days during the tour's stop in Sweden shooting studio footage to go along with the live concert footage Lukas's cameramen had already taken.

"Wonder what that's all about," Star murmured to Tank under her breath.

Before Tank could answer, a loud, jangling, ringing sound came from somewhere nearby. Glancing over, Star realized it was the brass-plated telephone sitting on a polished marble-and-brass end table beside one of the suite's leather sofas.

"You got that, Mags?" Tank asked, nodding toward Mike, who was glancing helplessly at the ringing phone while still pressing the cell phone to his ear.

The tutor stepped over and scooped up the phone. "Good evening," she said briskly. "May I help you?"

Star was so tired that it made her feel a little dizzy to glance back and forth from Mike to Mags. She sank to the floor in a crouching position, patting Dudley, who eagerly pressed himself against her legs. Mike was still murmuring quietly into his cell, but Mags's clear, no-nonsense voice rang out clearly.

"I'm sorry, young lady," she said into the phone in her best don't-question-me tone. "I'm afraid I can't help you with that. Miss Calloway is very busy. But I'm sure she greatly appreciates your support. Good night."

"Was that a fan or something, Mrs. Nattle?" Star asked as her tutor hung up the phone. She felt a familiar flash of slightly wistful guilt. From the time she had become famous, Star had wished she could answer all of the calls from her fans, respond to all of their letters and e-mails, take the time to meet each of them personally. But Mike and the others had soon helped her to see that it was just impossible. Star had millions of fans—even saying hello to all of them would take up more hours than there were in a year. If she wanted to get anything else done—like recording new songs, going on tour, sleeping, and eating—it meant she had to ignore most of the fans clamoring for her attention. She accepted that, though she still didn't like it.

Mags nodded. "It was a girl about your age—American accent," she said. "She claimed to be an old chum from kindergarten or some such."

"Really?" Star said, vaguely recalling other fans who had tried similar tricks in the past. Still, she couldn't resist asking, "What's her name?"

"Sam," Mags replied. "Short for Samantha, presumably. She didn't mention her surname."

Star scanned a long mental list of friends and acquaintances from back home, her tired mind seeming to work in slow motion. Finally she shrugged. "I don't think I remember any Sams. Except the guy who mows Nans's lawn for her, and he's like forty years old."

"I'm sure it was just another fan saying whatever she thought it would take to get to meet you," Tank said. "Don't worry about it, Star-baby."

Star nodded, leaning back against a beige plaster pillar. It always seemed weird to her that people she didn't know would go to such lengths just for a moment or two of her attention. What was it about being famous that suddenly made everything she did and said so interesting to total strangers?

I totally remember how it is, though, she thought sleepily. *Wishing like crazy that I could meet some of my idols—I mean, if I'd known three years ago that I would actually be personally acquainted with Eddie Urbane, or Lukas Lukas, or the guys from Boysterous, I'm sure I would have gone crazy. . . .*

Mike hung up his cell phone and tucked it into his shirt pocket. "Well, well," he said, sounding surprised but happy. "Seems Star's latest video is going to kick things off on that new show the gang from PopTV is premiering in a few days."

Star snapped out of her sleepy musings. She'd almost forgotten about her manager's conversation with Lukas Lukas.

"What do you mean? What did Mr. Lukas say?" she asked, giving Dudley one last pat as she stood up and stepped toward Mike.

"Is this about that show they've been pushing on PopTV for the past couple of weeks?" Lola asked, leaving her packing long enough to hurry over and join the others. "There's been an ad for it about every five minutes—*In This Moment,* I think it's called. Supposed to be the hottest brand-new videos plus all sorts of other trendy stuff."

"That's the one." Mike stroked his mustache. "We got a call from them earlier today—seems the combo of our Star and the Swedish genius has the PopTV folks drooling. They think premiering "Blast from the Past" during their first episode will really get folks tuning in."

"They're right." Lola spoke up immediately, stepping over and giving Star a hug. "Everyone wants a piece of our girl. And who can blame them?"

Star laughed and hugged her back. "Thanks, Lola." She glanced at Mike. "But is the video going to be finished in time?"

"That's what Lukas was calling about," Mike replied. "He thinks he can do it. He's going to work around the clock so it's ready. Lucky for us over half the video is going to be concert footage—makes it a little easier, I reckon."

"Cool," Star said. "I can't wait to see how it turns out."

Her last words were nearly swallowed in a huge yawn that seemed to come out of nowhere.

"You okay?" Mike asked with concern. "You look a little tired. Want to head off to bed and let us finish up here?"

"No, I'm fine," Star responded quickly. World-famous or not, she wasn't about to make her team do her share of the work just because she was tired. "Just tell me what to do."

Mike looked skeptical, but he pointed to a trio of boxes

standing beside several large, messy stacks of paperwork. "All right then," he said. "Those file folders need packing."

"I'm on it."

Star hurried over to the file folder boxes with Dudley at her heels. She kneeled down in front of the first one and grabbed a handful of papers off the top of the nearest stack.

"Look out, Dudley," she warned the pug as he stood up on his hind legs and peered into the box. "I need to get in there."

In response, the little dog hopped over the edge of the box, landing inside among the metal file brackets. He sat down and looked up at Star, seeming to smile at her as his tongue lolled out of his mouth.

Star rolled her eyes and giggled. "Get out of there, Dudster," she ordered. "Come on—now."

She grabbed the little dog and tried to lift him out of the box. But Dudley braced his hind legs against the sides of the box, making it impossible to pull him out without bringing the entire bracket frame with him.

"Doing all right, Star?" Mags asked, glancing down at her as she hurried past.

"No problem," Star told her with a sigh.

She decided that the best way to ensure that Dudley got

bored with his game was to ignore him. Turning to the second file box, she quickly filled it with papers from the stacks.

Someone had already organized the papers, which meant that it was pretty boring work—all Star had to do was grab one section, then drop it into the matching folder. Soon her eyes were glazing over, and she was yawning.

Almost done, she thought, shaking her head to clear the cloudy, pillowy cobwebs of sleepiness that were drifting through her mind and making it hard to focus. *As soon as everything's packed, we can all get some sleep. . . .*

She turned to grab the next handful of papers. As she did, her sleepy, unfocused gaze skittered over the phone on the end table. She thought about that call from her fan—Sam? Was that her name?

I wonder who she is, Star thought drowsily. She grabbed the lid to one of the boxes and slid it into place. *I wonder if she came to any of my concerts here in Germany. Or maybe she was calling from somewhere else. If we weren't leaving first thing in the morning, I bet Mike would already be complaining to the hotel switchboard about putting the call through. . . .*

She grabbed the second lid. As she pushed it onto one of the file boxes, she heard a muffled yelp.

"What was that?" Mike asked, glancing up from his own packing job nearby.

Star blinked and glanced down at the box. It was wriggling back and forth on the floor. Another, more irritated-sounding yip came from inside.

"Oops," Star said sheepishly, peeling off the lid. As soon as she did, Dudley's head popped up and he glared at her. "Sorry about that, Dudster," she said, grabbing the little dog. This time he allowed her to pull him free of the box.

Mike chuckled. "Okay, that settles it," he said. "If you're too tired to notice you're filing your dog, you're too tired to stay up any longer."

"But I want to help!" Star protested weakly.

"No deal," Mike replied firmly. He pointed toward the door to Star's bedroom at the far end of the suite. "Off to bed. And that's an order."

Star opened her mouth to protest, then realized he was right. She was too tired to be of any use, anyway.

"Thanks, Mike," she said with relief, dragging herself to her feet. "Good night, everyone. See you in the morning."

She headed into her bedroom with Dudley at her heels. The room was small but elegantly furnished in shades of white and beige. Shutting the door behind her, she collapsed onto the fluffy feather bed as dizzying waves of weariness washed over her.

Not wanting to fall asleep right there in her clothes, she forced her eyes open and sat up. Dudley was sniffing around at the suitcases containing Star's traveling clothes and personal items, which were already mostly packed.

Star quickly changed into her nightgown, then crawled back into bed. Her laptop was sitting on the bedside table. Even as sleepy as she was, she couldn't resist grabbing it. Being so far away from home for so long, her computers— the laptop and the tiny handheld she kept in her purse— were her best link to her friends back home.

She quickly logged on and opened her e-mail. Spotting a message from Missy Takamori, her best friend, she clicked on it. Missy and several of Star's other friends from home had flown to Europe for a visit recently. Lukas Lukas had even invited them to be extras in the "Blast from the Past" video shoot. Star couldn't wait to tell Missy and the others about the video's premiere on PopTV.

Missy's message popped up, and Star leaned forward to scan it.

From: MissTaka

To: singingstar0l

Subject: yay and neigh!

Yo Star,

Guess what??? Remember how I told u my mom&dad were threatening 2 send me back 2 math camp this yr? Well, I guess they finally realized it's a lost cause. Cuz they just told me I can go 2 horseback riding camp instead!!!!!!!!!! Can u believe it??? After all those yrs of begging, they're finally going 2 let me learn 2 ride! Camp starts next month, & I'm already counting the days . . .

:-D

Love, yr happy bff,

Missy (future horsewoman!)

Star leaned back against the pillows without typing an answer, feeling oddly unsettled. How many times had she and Missy talked and schemed and dreamed together, planning to take riding lessons together someday? She couldn't even count that high.

And now she's going to do it without me, Star thought.

She felt a twinge of some emotion she couldn't quite recognize as she thought back to her own mother's many tales of growing up riding ponies with her best friends. Somehow Star had assumed that she would learn to ride someday too. And she had assumed she would do it with Missy.

But that's not too likely to happen, I guess, Star realized, biting her lip. *I mean, it's not like I could just go off to camp like a normal kid even if I wasn't touring all summer. . . .*

The thought made her feel sad all of a sudden, even though she knew it was silly. It wasn't as if she'd trade her current life of doing what she loved for all the riding lessons in the world. And it wasn't as if she blamed Missy one bit for going ahead and doing what she wanted.

Still, thinking about her best friend starting a fun new adventure without her made that familiar ache of homesickness start up again in the pit of Star's stomach. Mike had always warned her that becoming a superstar would mean giving up a lot of things that most people took for granted. She was starting to understand what he meant.

She quickly typed out a brief response to Missy—"Cool news! Way tired; will write more l8r"—and hit send. As soon as the message went through, she turned off the computer and set it back on the side table.

Then she sighed and leaned back against the silk-cased

down pillows on the bed. She closed her eyes and felt Dudley's familiar weight settling into place on her feet.

It's just a few days until I get to go home for that visit, she told herself as the gray, fuzzy shadows of sleep drifted in from the corners of her mind. *I'm sure that will make me feel much better—about everything.*

Two

"Wow." Star stared out the tour bus window at the odd-looking building looming directly ahead. "When you guys said this was a theme hotel, you weren't kidding!"

The bus was driving slowly up a long, straight avenue lined with fake palm trees. As they drew closer a gate shaped like a miniature Mount Rushmore split open between Thomas Jefferson and Theodore Roosevelt, allowing the bus to pull onto a curving drive that circled a flagstone courtyard in front of the main hotel building. There were three flagpoles in the center of the courtyard. The pole on the left flew a small Swiss flag. The one on the right held a small red-white-and-blue flag with the words "The American Hotel— Zurich" on it. In the middle, on a much taller pole, fluttered the largest American flag Star had ever seen.

But Star's attention flickered quickly past the flags. She was much more interested in the building itself, which looked as if someone had taken every famous structure or monument in the United States and tossed them all into a blender. The front entrance of the sprawling hotel resembled the facade of the Capitol Building in Washington, D.C. One wing seemed to be an uneasy fusion of Independence Hall in Philadelphia and the New York Stock Exchange, and on the other side a larger wing combined a Southern plantation house with an Old West–style saloon and the Astrodome. The upper stories of the hotel sprouted off into several different towers meant to copy famous American skyscrapers—the Sears Tower, the Empire State Building, and a couple of others Star didn't immediately recognize. Standing proudly atop it all was a half-scale model of the Statue of Liberty with the famous Hollywood sign spilling across her crown.

Mike was sitting beside Star at the table in the bus's kitchenette going through some paperwork. Leaning over her, he glanced out the window and groaned.

"Jumpin' Jehosephat," he said. "Looks even worse than the picture on the Web site." He shrugged. "Never mind, though. It's supposed to have the best security team in Switzerland. That's why we're here."

Star grinned. "If the inside is as wild as the outside, I think it'll be a blast!" she said. "I was getting tired of all those stuffy, elegant beige suites anyway."

"You said it, sister," Lola agreed with a laugh. "Everybody needs a little kitsch once in a while."

"A little?" Mags peered out the window as they drove past a section of lawn scattered with pink flamingos.

Glancing again at the flag courtyard, Star noticed a semi-circle of life-size statues surrounding the flagpoles. Several people were standing among them posing for photos.

"Okay, I recognize George Washington and Marilyn Monroe," Star said, pointing out one statue after another. "And I guess that's probably supposed to be Joe DeMaggio or somebody over there next to Benjamin Franklin. But who the heck are those two on the end?"

Mags rolled her eyes and sighed. "Oh, dear," she said. "Perhaps we've been studying too much European history lately at the expense of American history. Otherwise you would know that of course those two statues are meant to represent Lewis and Clark."

"Oops." Star giggled sheepishly. "Sorry, Mrs. Nattle. I do remember who they are—you made me write an essay on them last year during that publicity tour through the Midwest, remember? I just didn't recognize them standing next to Mickey Mouse."

The bus pulled to a stop in front of the lobby entrance. "End of the line," Tank called from behind the wheel.

Star looked out the window and saw several burly men hurrying toward the bus. "Check out the security guards," she said with a giggle.

Mike walked forward and stepped off the bus to greet the guards as Mags and Lola peered out the window. "Oh, my," Mags said.

Lola grinned. "Awesome," she said. "Who knew that Alfred Hitchcock, Jesse James, and Elvis were all still alive and working for a hotel in Switzerland?"

Star laughed and leaned over to retrieve Dudley, who was snoozing under the table. "Come on, Duds," she said, tweaking his ear to wake him up. "Time to check in."

Thanks to the hotel guards, who turned out to be polite and efficient despite their goofy uniforms, it was only a matter of minutes before Star was standing in the enormous hotel lobby waiting for Mike to finish talking with the check-in staff. She tipped her head back to take in the vaulted ceiling, which featured scenes from the American space program, including a dangling replica of the space shuttle.

"Wow," she commented to Lola, who was standing beside her. "This place is really nuts."

"No kidding, honey," Lola agreed, glancing around. "I love it!"

Star grinned. "Me too!"

The lobby was just as outrageous as the outside of the hotel building. The security guards weren't the only employees wearing costumes—the bellman who had held the door for them was dressed as a cowboy, the man at the check-in counter wore a New York Yankees uniform, and a maid sweeping up near the entrance to the restaurant bore a startling resemblance to Pocahontas. The wall behind the counter held a brightly colored mural depicting a battle between cowboys and Indians, and poster-size photos of Hollywood celebrities, sports figures, and American politicians decorated the wall behind a spacious seating area nearby. At the far end of the lobby, to one side of the elevator bank leading to the rooms upstairs, was a neon-lit diner counter, looking completely authentic right down to the gum-snapping waitresses in pink uniforms and the fresh apple pie in the dessert case.

There were about a dozen other hotel guests in the lobby, and a few stared as they recognized Star, but no one approached the group. Star wondered if that was because Swiss people were reserved and polite, as she'd heard, or if it had more to do with Tank's imposing presence immediately behind her.

As Star gazed at the wall of TVs, which were playing all kinds of old American programs, Mike strode toward her. "Y'all ready to head upstairs?" he asked. "They have us in two separate suites, but apparently they're joined by a—"

"Entshuldigen Sie bitte," an expensively dressed woman interrupted, hurrying over and tapping Mike on the arm. She immediately launched into a torrent of some foreign language, spoken so rapidly that Star couldn't even figure out what language it was.

Mike stared at the stranger helplessly, then glanced at Tank, who was standing nearby. "Little help here?" he said.

"She's speaking Greek," Tank said. "Mixed in with a little German. I guess she thinks you're part of the staff."

Star blinked in surprise. Despite his laid-back demeanor, Mike had a naturally strong presence that commanded respect everywhere he went. She couldn't remember ever seeing him mistaken for anyone other than the person in charge.

Lola laughed. "Go figure." She pointed toward Mike's feet.

Along with the others, Star stared at her manager's purple cowboy boots, which he wore everywhere. Then her eyes moved upward to take in the rest of his outfit. That particular day he had dressed for comfort on the long bus ride; above the boots he wore a pair of well-faded blue jeans with a silver rodeo buckle at his waist, a souvenir of a brief teenage career as a bull rider.

Mike scowled at Lola and Tank, who were grinning from ear to ear. Even Mags seemed to be trying to hide a smile.

Star giggled. "Don't worry, Mike," she said. "You look much more authentic than that doorman. His belt buckle probably isn't even from a real rodeo."

"Okay, okay," Mike said sourly. "Tank, could you please deal with this situation?"

"Sure thing." Tank turned to the woman, who was beginning to look confused and slightly annoyed. Giving a slight bow, he spoke to her in her own language.

Star had no idea what her bodyguard was saying. But after a moment the woman turned and gazed at her curiously.

"Ah!" the stranger said in tentative English. "Star Calloway. Yes, the young American singer. Why, you are even more pretty in person, my dear!"

"Hello," Star said with a polite smile. "Thank you very much."

"All right then," Mike said. "Now that that's settled . . ."

He took Star's arm and steered her toward the elevators. The rest of the group followed. A hotel employee dressed as Abraham Lincoln was waiting to usher them into one of the elevators.

Just as Star was about to follow Mags into the elevator, she heard a man's voice shouting her name. She glanced back, expecting to see a fan clamoring for an autograph.

Instead it was another hotel employee. This one was costumed as a surfer. He wore flip-flops and shorts, along with a Hawaiian shirt with a palm-and-parrot pattern so loud that Star's eyes almost crossed just looking at it. He also had a small but brightly colored surfboard tucked under one arm.

"Pardon," the man said, holding out a note with the hand that wasn't busy holding the surfboard. "I have here a very important message for Miss Calloway. The young lady insisted that I be certain to deliver it personally."

"Thank you." Mike accepted the note and unfolded it as the employee hurried away.

Star stepped into the elevator. "Who's it from?" she asked as Mike glanced down at the sheet. "It's not from Lukas Lukas, is it? There's no problem with the video after all, I hope?"

"No, nothing like that," Mike said. "Just says there was a

call for you before we arrived. Young lady named Samantha Bradley."

"Samantha?" Mags repeated. "That's the name of the girl who called us in Germany yesterday."

Star nodded. "What else did she say?"

Mike glanced at the note again. "Just that she lives here in Zurich now, but that she knows you from back home," he said. "Same business as last night, more or less. That you two went to kindergarten together and you'll know who she is."

"Ringing any bells?" Tank asked Star.

"Samantha Bradley . . . Samantha Bradley . . ." Star searched her mind. But no matter how hard she thought, she couldn't recall anyone by that name. "Nope," she said at last. "I don't think so. Not that I can remember, anyway."

"Good enough." Mike crumpled the note in his fist and shoved it into his pocket.

Soon they were all stepping into the first of their two adjoining suites. "Hmm," Mike commented, taking a slow look around. "Guess they weren't kidding when they called this the presidential suite."

Star set Dudley down on the parquet floor. "Is this supposed to look like the White House or something?" she asked, taking in the framed presidential portraits on the walls and the impressive, highly polished furniture.

"Oval Office, to be specific." Tank pointed to the curving wall at the far end of the room.

Star hurried to peer through the doorways into the other rooms. The suite had three bedrooms, each featuring portraits and paraphernalia from a different well-known U.S. president. The spacious bathroom was dedicated to first ladies through the years.

Tank followed her, peering over her shoulder into each room. "Lincoln bedroom, anyone?" he said. "Or maybe you're in more of a Washington mood. What do you think, Star-baby?"

"Actually, I was sort of hoping for something more exciting," Star said. "These bedrooms look way too much like the rest of the stuffy hotels we've been staying in. Come on, let's check out the other suite—maybe that one's more fun. Who has the keys?"

"Right here." Mike tossed one of the card keys to Lola. "That one's called the Wild West suite. I don't even want to know what it looks like."

"Well, I do." Lola led the way toward the adjoining door. "Come on, gang."

Tank was in front of Star as Lola unlocked the door, so at

first she couldn't see a thing around his substantial bulk.

"Whoa!" Lola said from in front of Tank. "Check this place out!"

"What?" Star asked eagerly, poking Tank in the back to encourage him to move faster. "What's it like? Let me see!"

Tank stepped through the door and moved aside. Star hurried forward, almost tripping over Dudley, who was standing at her feet, and gasped as she got a look at the suite's main room.

"Wow!" she exclaimed, breaking into a grin. "Now, *this* is what I call a hotel room!"

Stepping into the Wild West suite felt like striding into a frontier saloon. Instead of the usual tasteful beige upholstery or elegant antiques, the main room featured rough-hewn wooden beams, rustic log chairs, and a long, polished wooden bar at one end of the room. While Star caught hints of modern conveniences here and there—a microwave glimpsed through the swinging doors leading to the kitchenette, a big-screen TV set into the mirrored wall above the bar—she was impressed by all the interesting Western details. It was as if whoever had designed the suite had tried to include every detail from every American Western film ever made. But Star only had time for a cursory glance at all of that. As soon as her gaze wandered to the center of the room, it fixed on the full-size mechanical bull on a broad, low, well-padded platform.

Star gasped. In all her travels, she had never seen such a thing other than on TV. "Do you think it works?"

Lola stepped toward the contraption, bending over to peer at the control panel at the edge of the padded floor of the platform. "Knowing this place," she said, "I can almost guarantee it." She reached out and flipped a switch. With a crunching of gears, the bull started bucking and spinning. Dudley jumped in surprise, then leaped forward, barking valiantly at the mechanical creature.

"Way cool! I get to go first!" Star cried.

"No, me!" Lola protested. "Age before beauty, babydoll."

Tank rolled his eyes. "Stand aside, ladies," he said with a mock swagger. "Let this here cowboy show you how it's done."

Star giggled. "No way," she said. "I called it first. That means I—"

"Star! Darling!" The playful argument was interrupted by a loud, nasal voice with a strong New York accent.

Star turned as her head publicist, Tricia Moore, blasted into the suite from the adjoining room, her high heels clicking on the wooden floorboards. As usual Tricia sported a stylish pantsuit, bright red lipstick, and short-cropped magenta hair. She didn't so much as spare a glance at the unusual decor, striding straight up to Star and bending down slightly to talk to her eye to eye.

"Darling!" Tricia said briskly, her breath tickling Star's face and smelling of coffee and breath mints. "I have fabulous news. The 'Blast from the Past' video premiere is all set. I just confirmed it with Lukas's people."

"That's great," Star said politely, even though the news wasn't terribly surprising. "Thanks, Tricia."

"But that's not all." Tricia playfully waggled one scarlet fingernail in Star's face. "I've also arranged a premiere party right here in Switzerland—you know, just a bit more publicity for the big event. It will coincide with the premiere broadcast, and PopTV has already promised to send a camera crew to cover it—they want to show you live as part of the show, partying down right along with your fans." She rubbed her hands together briskly, an eager gleam in her eyes. "The entertainment press back home should eat that up."

Star glanced up at Mike, who had just entered the room. "Sounds good to me," she said. "Is that going to be okay with my schedule?"

Mike nodded, stroking his mustache. "I'm working it out, sweetheart," he said. "Luckily you don't have a concert that evening. But thanks to the time difference between here and New York, we'll have to rearrange a couple of things so you can actually get some sleep that night."

"Cool." Realizing that her team had everything under control as usual, Star was already shifting her attention back to the mechanical bull. Tank had switched it off when Tricia entered, but Lola was still standing near the control panel. "Want to get ready to crank that up so I can go for a ride?" Star asked the stylist with a grin. "Tank can give me a leg up."

She took a step toward the bull. But Mike put a hand on her shoulder to stop her. "Sorry, Star," he said. "There's no time for messin' around right now. You're due at a lunch meeting with some sponsors in less than an hour, with a choreography meeting right after. Then there's the concert tonight, and you've got a full schedule tomorrow. You're going to be busier'n a hound in flea season for the next twenty four."

"Not to mention your schoolwork," Mags spoke up. "In case you've forgotten, we've missed quite a few lessons lately, what with last-minute video shoots and sudden visits from friends and such. We need to get back on schedule, or you'll still be attempting to work your way through high school when you're Mike's age."

"I know, Mrs. Nattle," Star said. "I promise I'm going to work hard this week—I already started reading that history chapter on Napoleon on the bus this morning, remember?"

She tried to keep the disappointment out of her voice. Her team was only doing what was best for her—guiding her career and helping her grow as an artist and as a person. Maybe that meant missing out on a little spontaneous fun once in a while, but she'd known that when she signed on for this lifestyle. In exchange for lazy summer days of doing whatever she wanted, of going to horseback riding camp with her best friend or following an impulse to try something new, she had all the money and fame she ever could have imagined, not to mention the chance to do what she loved more than anything else in the world. That seemed like a pretty fair trade to her—at least, most of the time.

Stepping forward just long enough to give the mechanical bull a quick pat, she sighed and followed Mike out of the room.

Three

"Napoleon, Napoleon," Star murmured, trying to keep her gaze focused on the page in front of her.

She was sprawled on the bed in one of the rooms in the Wild West suite, her European history textbook propped against a pillow. Mags had warned that she would be giving Star a pop quiz on the Napoleon chapter sometime in the next few days, and Star wanted to be ready. She had always taken pride in the good grades she'd earned in school, and she knew her parents had always been proud of them too.

When she'd shot to superstardom with the release of her first album about a year earlier, she had realized that her school days were over. Thanks to Mags, though, Star was keeping up with her former schoolmates. Mike was careful to allow the two of them plenty of quality time each week, which they spent studying in the meeting room of her pied-à-terre back in New York, visiting various museums, libraries, and other educational sites around the city, or tucked into Nans Calloway's den in New Limpet.

But it hadn't taken long for her to realize that studying while on tour was going to be more challenging than Star had expected. Her hectic life was even less predictable on the road, with a new hotel in a new city every few days, a tight concert schedule, and more interviews, publicity stops, and photo shoots than ever. Mags had adjusted Star's curriculum to take advantage of their history-soaked European surroundings, and Mike made sure to set off blocks of free time here and there, but it remained difficult to stay on schedule. Star found herself doing much of her schoolwork on the tour bus, or in the bathtub, or at other odd moments here and there. Sometimes it was hard to make herself open up a textbook after a long day of interviews and photo shoots, let alone after a concert, which always left her happy but exhausted. But she did her best to find the energy to keep up as best she could. The last thing she wanted to do was disappoint her tutor—or her parents, whenever they returned.

That particular day, however, the more she tried to concentrate on the page in front of her, the harder it was to keep her attention from wandering to more immediate concerns. Looking at all the battle pictures of Napoleon on horseback reminded her of Missy's e-mail about riding camp. And the details of her room didn't help—the bedside table was made out of a real Western saddle, and there was a life-size mural of grazing horses covering one wall.

Finally Star sat up and pushed the history textbook away. Swinging her legs over the edge of the bed, she reached for her laptop. Someone had unpacked for her while she was at her lunch meeting with some Swiss business executives, and the computer was sitting on the saddle table along with Star's diary and her favorite framed photo of her family.

Soon she was clicking on her e-mail in-box. There were several new messages, but none showed Missy's familiar return address.

Star sighed, her fingers wandering up to fiddle with her star necklace. She knew she should write to her friend again, offer some sincere congratulations on her good news. But she couldn't quite bring herself to do it—not just yet. Instead she scanned the list of new messages. One showed the return address "SuperStarCFan."

"Wendall," she murmured with a smile.

Twelve-year-old Wendall Wiggins had written Star the very first fan letter she'd ever received, and he still considered himself her number-one fan. He ran Star's most popular fan Web site, named after her first album, *Star Power*. Wendall lived in New York City and Star had met him several times there, usually when he turned out to see her at a publicity appearance. Just seeing his wild red hair and eager freckled face in a crowd always made her smile.

Star clicked on the message.

From: SuperStarCFan

To: singingstar0I

Subject: Your beautiful face

Dear Star,

I hope ur having a wonderful tour! If only I could get tix to every I of ur concerts all across the world, I wd b the happiest boy ever 2 live. But alas! My evil 'rents won't support my plans 2 drop out of school to follow u everywhere. o well . . .

So I thought u might like 2 check out the new pix I just put up on the site. As always, u look like a beautiful vision of perfection in every I of them. I hope u like them!

Your most devoted fan,

Wendall P. Wiggins

Star hit SAVE so she could answer Wendall's note later. Then she clicked on a saved link, and within seconds the Star Power site's familiar logo, a picture of Star holding a microphone, was loading. Star quickly followed another link to the photo page and checked out the new pictures Wendall had mentioned.

"Yick," she murmured as she noticed a small photo near the bottom of the page. It was an action shot of her at a fashion show she'd recently attended. She was standing up at the edge of the catwalk, her mouth half open and her blue eyes half closed.

She sighed. Wendell seemed to think that every picture that featured her was a masterpiece. She knew he would delete the photo if she asked, but it didn't seem worth the effort. She had been terribly embarrassed the first few times a photographer had caught her in an unflattering pose, but by now she was used to it.

She knew she should log off and go back to her studying. But she couldn't resist clicking on another link on the page. She liked to keep up with what her fans were thinking, and the Star Power site's busy message board was an easy way to do so.

She scrolled quickly down the long list of new messages. Judging from the subject lines, many of the threads seemed to concern recent rumors linking Star romantically with fellow teen pop star Eddie Urbane. Many others involved the ongoing search for Star's missing family, while the rest were mostly comments or questions about her tour, new album, or recent videos.

Then she stopped short, her finger frozen on the mouse pad, as a different subject line caught her eye.

Topic: MY OLD FRIEND STAR!!!
Author: SAMIAM

Star blinked. "Sam I am," she whispered. "Sam—like Samantha?" She wondered if it was a coincidence, or if the message could have something to do with the girl who had tried to contact her in Germany and here in Switzerland.

Clicking on the message, she saw that it was a repeat of the note from that morning. It included a plea to Star herself—"if u r reading this"—to please get in touch, and was signed Samantha Bradley.

"So it is the same person," Star murmured, sitting back and staring at the glowing screen.

She couldn't help being intrigued. Was it possible this Samantha Bradley really was an old friend from way back when?

Or was it more likely that SamIAm was just an especially crazed fan—maybe even some kind of stalker? Star shivered as she recalled a story she'd heard recently while on a long plane ride with Eddie Urbane. Eddie loved to talk about himself, and at one point his ongoing monologue had turned to the subject of his stalkers, past and present. He made it sound as if countless rabid fans of his were sitting in jail or on the other end of restraining orders because of their crazed attacks or other illegal behavior.

Star knew that stalkers could be a serious problem for some celebrities. Mike had had a few talks with her about the possibilities, mostly after Star had ignored his warnings about leaving her New York apartment alone—but she also knew that most of what Eddie Urbane had to say was exaggerated if not totally made up.

Maybe Samantha really does know me from years ago, and maybe not, she told herself. *If not, though, she's probably just another super-enthusiastic fan. And I love those!*

"Thanks, everybody! You've been great! Good night!"

Star gave one last wave and bounced off the concert stage to the final flourishes of her band's exit music. Her face was flushed, her heart was pumping, and she felt great.

"Awesome job tonight, Star," Erin Maxwell said, pausing to give Star a friendly clap on the back as the dancers hurried offstage. "I can't believe that high note you hit in 'Someday, Some Way.' You sounded great!"

"Thanks." Star peeled off her headset and handed it to a waiting tech. "I guess I got a little carried away there—that run just seemed to appear out of nowhere, and I went with it."

"I loved it," Rachel said, appearing at her sister's shoulder. "I think you should sing it that way from now on." She glanced over and spotted Mike striding in their direction. "No matter what Mr. Cowboy says about it," she added in a whisper, with a mischievous wink.

Star giggled. All of the dancers loved to tease Mike about his cowboy boots and Texas accent, but she knew they adored him almost as much as she did. As Rachel and Erin scurried off to their dressing room, she turned and waited for Mike to reach her.

"Sounded good tonight, darlin'," Mike said, reaching down to give her a hug. "Real good. Ready to get out of costume and get out of here? You need to be up early tomorrow for that morning-show radio interview, and I don't want you yawnin' your way through it."

"Okay," Star said. "Is Lola in my dressing room? I can't get out of this thing without her help." She gestured at the star-spangled, glow-in-the-dark costume she was wearing, which involved an elaborate zipper and snap system in the back.

Mike grinned behind his bushy mustache. "She's waitin' there with a crowbar and a blowtorch, I think," he said. "So scoot. Tank and I'll meet you two by the back door."

Less than half an hour later Star was walking toward the back entrance of the stadium with Mike on one side and Tank on the other. Lola trailed behind them, and several other bodyguards walked ahead, prepared to clear the way through the inevitable crowd of fans and reporters outside. Star had removed her stage costume along with most of her makeup, and she was dressed in jeans and a cute top. Even though she was heading straight back to the hotel, Lola had carefully reapplied just enough makeup to Star's face to make her look fresh and photogenic, as well as pulling her curly blonde hair into a perky ponytail with a pink scrunchie. One of the first things Star had learned when she became famous was that her days of going out in public in sloppy, comfortable sweatpants with messy hair were over. She always had to be ready to face the cameras that awaited her everywhere she went.

Sure enough, as soon as the door opened, cameras flashed

like fireflies and the warm night air was filled with frantic shouts as the photographers jostled one another, trying to get Star's attention. Star glanced over the crowd, being careful not to squint despite the bright flashes going off in front of her face. The crowd was gathered behind two sets of blue velvet ropes strung between metal poles, which left a narrow aisle across the sidewalk from the backstage door to the limo waiting at the curb. Although the ropes alone wouldn't have held the eager onlookers and photographers back for one second, the burly security guards and stern-looking local police officers standing guard along the length of the ropes looked much more daunting. Even so, the moment Star had appeared in the doorway the crowd surged forward, and now the guards were staying busy trying to keep anyone from pushing through or ducking under the ropes.

"Stay back!" Tank shouted in his deepest and most authoritative voice, putting a protective arm on Star's shoulder. "Please let us through." Since Switzerland had four national languages, he quickly repeated the commands in each of them: German, French, Italian, and Romansh.

Meanwhile Mike took Star's other arm and steered her down the narrow aisle. About halfway to the limo he paused and leaned down. "Let's give them a quick photo op, sweetheart, okay?" he whispered into her ear.

Star nodded. As Mike took a few steps back, she turned to face the crowd on one side. "Hello, everyone," she called, flashing her most brilliant smile. "Thanks for your support."

She held still, just as Lola had taught her, allowing the photographers a moment to capture her image. Then she turned around, ready to repeat the process for the other half of the crowd.

"Star! Star!" A shrill voice broke through the clamor before Star could speak again. "Over here! It's me, Sam!"

Star blinked. She glanced toward the source of the voice and immediately spotted a short, brown-haired girl around her age struggling to push past several adult photographers who were surging forward with their cameras at the ready.

"Okay, one more smile and wave, then let's get out of here," Mike prompted Star, glancing at his watch. "It's not gettin' any earlier."

"Just a sec," Star said distractedly. She was still peering at the girl, who was desperately elbowing a tall photographer in the ribs as he tried to squeeze her out. Star hated seeing the way her fans so often got shuffled to the back of the line by overly aggressive photographers and reporters. It didn't seem fair that the kids who supported her career, who spent their own money to buy her albums and attend her concerts, usually got stuck behind a bunch of greedy, pushy paparazzi who didn't care whom they trampled on the way to the perfect celebrity photo.

Star stepped toward the rope. There was a swelling of noise as the gathered crowd gasped at her approach, but she had eyes only for the brown-haired girl.

"Hold it, Star-baby!" Tank sounded startled as he stepped forward to keep her from reaching the edge of the crowd. "Where do you think you're going?"

Star barely heard him. "Hey," she said to the tall photographer. "Be careful. You're hurting her." She gestured to the girl.

The photographer looked surprised and slightly annoyed, but he stepped aside. The girl grabbed the rope with both hands and smiled at Star. "Thanks, Star," she said in American-accented English. "I was trying like crazy to get your attention, and that guy just kept shoving me!"

"You're welcome," Star said, returning her smile. "Thanks for coming tonight, and I hope you enjoyed the show."

She prepared to move on, but the girl pushed against the rope, reaching toward her. Tank immediately stepped between the two of them, gesturing to the nearest policeman.

"Wait!" the girl called, scrabbling against Tank's broad

back to peer around him. "Star, hold on a minute! Don't you remember me? It's me—Sam! Samantha Bradley! From New Limpet!"

Star blinked in surprise. "Sam?" she said. "From the notes?"

"Never mind, Star," Mike said, sounding slightly alarmed. "Come on, I think it's time we get while the gettin's good."

"No, please!" Sam called, her voice ringing out over the continuing cries and murmurs of the crowd. "You have to believe me. We totally know each other, I swear! Don't you remember how I used to come over to your house to play with you and Missy?"

Star gasped at the mention of her best friend's name. "Missy?" she said. "You really know Missy?"

"Sure!" A hopeful note entered Sam's voice. "Missy Takamori. We were all in Ms. Foster's kindergarten class together at New Limpet Elementary. It's true, you have to believe me! I can prove it—the school's on Grove Street, and—"

"Mike!" Star exclaimed, not needing to hear anymore. "Did you hear that? She really does know me!"

"Wait, Star," Mike began.

But Star was already rushing back toward the rope. She pushed a startled Tank aside. "Come on, duck under," she said, grabbing the other girl's hand. "I want to talk to you."

The crowd shrieked with amazement, and Tank and the other security personnel leaped into action, trying to hold back the excited onlookers and keep more of them from crossing the ropes. Meanwhile Star pulled Sam into the open aisle and turned to face her curiously.

"So it's true?" she asked. "We really did know each other way back when?"

Sam nodded. "Don't you remember?"

"I'm sorry," Star said sincerely. "I guess I just don't. Maybe you could remind me? What kinds of stuff did we do together?"

Sam smiled. "Everything," she said, reaching up to adjust the headband holding back her long hair, which had been knocked slightly askew in her scuffle with the photographer. "I'd come over, and we'd play hide-and-seek or kick the can with a whole bunch of kids from your neighborhood. Then we'd all usually go to your house and your mom would give us some of her awesome banana brownies."

Star's heart jumped. "You remember my mom?" She instantly flashed back to her younger days, when her mother always seemed to have a plate of cookies or other freshly baked treats to offer Star's many friends. The banana brownies were everybody's special favorite—Star's mouth started to water just thinking about them.

Mike stepped forward and grabbed Star by the arm. "Listen, Star," he said tensely. "Things are gettin' kinda Western around here. We really need to go."

"Okay," Star said, suddenly snapping back to reality and realizing he was right. The photographers were still pushing against the security guards, and behind them, fans and curious onlookers were starting to get louder and rowdier. Still, she couldn't just leave this mysterious old friend who had suddenly appeared in front of her. "Can Sam come with us?" she asked Mike. "I need to talk to her some more."

"Sorry," Mike said firmly. "No can do."

Recognizing her manager's adamant tone, Star shot the other girl an apologetic glance. "Maybe we can get together tomorrow or something," she said. "Do you want to come to my hotel?"

"Sure!" Sam said eagerly.

"No," Mike said at the same moment. When Star looked up at him in surprise and disappointment, his stern expression softened. "Sorry, sweetheart, I just don't think that's such a fine idea," he said. He rubbed his chin, glancing toward Sam. "But I s'pose it probably wouldn't hurt for you two to hang out for a while somewhere else," he said. "If Miss Bradley here will leave a message at the front desk of the American with her phone number, I'll call her folks and set it up, okay?"

"Thanks, Mike!" Star cried, flinging her arms around him in an impulsive hug. "You're the best!"

"Come on, guys," Tank called urgently. "Let's move."

Star allowed Mike to pull her away toward the car. "See you tomorrow!" she called back to Sam. "I can't wait!"

Four

Star was so busy the next morning that she barely had time to breathe, let alone think about her upcoming meeting with the mysterious Samantha Bradley. After an early-morning radio interview, she had to rush off to attend a charity breakfast, followed by a costume fitting for an upcoming awards show, a meeting with a Swiss designer who wanted Star to promote a new line of running shoes, and another interview.

But Mike was as good as his word. After calling Samantha's parents to check out her story, he'd arranged to rent out a local restaurant for an hour or so. Sam would be meeting Star there for lunch.

Before she knew it, Star was sitting in the limo across from Mike on her way to the restaurant. She tapped her fingers anxiously on the armrest, staring out at the busy city streets and willing Tank to drive faster. She couldn't wait to spend some time with Samantha Bradley and find out more about their past together. If Sam remembered Mrs. Calloway's brownies so clearly, she probably remembered a whole lot more about Star's parents. And that was a topic Star never got tired of discussing.

"I'm still not sure this is such an all-fired wonderful idea," Mike commented, breaking into Star's thoughts as Tank steered the limo around a stopped bus. "Are you sure you want to go through with it? I can always call and cancel."

"No way," Star assured him. "I'm totally in."

Mike sighed, stroking his mustache. "Just wish I didn't have to go to this meeting about the PopTV premiere thing so I could stay with you. Hate leavin' you alone in this kind of situation."

"Situation?" Star laughed. "What kind of 'situation' is kicking back with an old friend? Don't worry, Mike. This isn't anything you have to chaperone. Just pretend I'm hanging with Missy for a couple of hours. It's basically the same thing, right?"

Mike shrugged. "Well, I dunno. But I called the girl's folks myself," he said. "Caught the mother on her way to a meeting and soundin' a little frazzled, but she did confirm that the family used to live in Pennsylvania. That call also confirmed that Ms. Bradley is a professor at the university here."

"See?" Star said with a smile. "Everything's cool. No problem."

Mike exchanged a glance with Tank in the rearview mirror. "Well, I s'pose there's not much can happen as long as Tank's with you," he said, still sounding a bit dubious. "Just let him know right away if anything feels uncomfortable. Just 'cause this girl knew where you went to kindergarten, it doesn't mean this couldn't still be a hoax."

"Okay." Star knew her manager was right. She was often surprised by how much her fans seemed to know about her. It was possible that Sam could have looked up all kinds of information about Star on the Internet and used that to concoct her story about knowing her.

But Star couldn't quite believe that. For one thing, there was the comment about the banana brownies. She was pretty sure that not even Mike or Mags or the rest of her team knew about those. The only ones who would remember such a thing would be her neighborhood friends and immediate family.

Besides, even if she didn't remember Sam, there was something about the other girl that made Star believe that the two of them might easily have been friends. Sam had a friendly, happy look in her eyes that made Star like her right away. You couldn't fake something like that.

Still, maybe it wouldn't hurt to ask her a few tricky questions when I see her, just to make sure, Star told herself as the limo pulled to the curb in front of a nondescript sandwich shop. *Like what color my bedroom was painted back then, or Missy's middle name . . .*

"Here we are," Tank announced, cutting the engine. "And it looks like nobody knew we were coming."

Glancing out the window, Star saw that for once there was no waiting crowd gathered to greet her. She was relieved. Still, she waited quietly for the two men to give her the okay to climb out of the car, only her constantly drumming fingers betraying her impatience.

Tank and Mike quickly traded places, Mike sliding into the driver's seat while Tank stood on the sidewalk outside the half-open window. "Page me if anything happens," Mike told Tank. "Otherwise I'll be back in an hour to pick you up."

"Got it," Tank said. "Come on, Star-baby."

He opened Star's door and helped her out. Then the two of them hurried into the restaurant, which consisted of two small rooms. The first room was dominated by a large glass display counter filled with delicious-looking luncheon meats, salads, and pastries. Behind it was a second room that held several tables. At the moment the only people present were Samantha Bradley, who was leaning against the glass counter, and a pair of women standing nearby who appeared to be the business's owners or employees.

"Star!" Sam cried eagerly, leaping forward as soon as Star entered. "You came! I was afraid you wouldn't."

She rushed forward, and Star reached out for an impulsive hug. Tank stood by, looking slightly nervous, but he didn't interfere as the two girls hugged each other tightly and then danced around in excitement.

"Of course I came!" Star laughed with delight at the other girl's enthusiasm. "I said I would, didn't I?"

Meanwhile one of the women stepped forward. "Excuse me," she said shyly in lightly accented English, nervously wiping her hands on her crisp white apron. "Miss Calloway, it is a great honor to have you here in my establishment. I—I wonder if I could trouble you for an autograph? My niece is a great fan of your music, and she would never forgive me if I did not ask."

"Sure!" Star said. "Tank?"

Her bodyguard reached into his jacket pocket, where he always carried a few publicity photographs for just such situations. He handed Star a photo, while the second employee scrambled to find a pen.

Sam watched as Star quickly signed a photo and handed it to the woman. "Wow," Sam said. "You did that just like a real celebrity!"

Star giggled. "Thanks. It wasn't my first time."

Soon the two girls were seated at a table in the corner of the back room out of sight of the windows. As the two women scurried back and forth, bringing sodas, glasses of water, and a variety of salads to the girls' table, Tank settled down at another table with a newspaper and a cup of coffee.

"Can he read that?" Sam whispered curiously, leaning across the table toward Star and gesturing at Tank.

"What do you mean?" Glancing over, Star saw that the newspaper her bodyguard was holding was written in German. She giggled. "Yep, he can read it," she confirmed. "Tank might look like a total meathead, but he's one of the smartest people I know. He speaks, like, seventeen languages, and knows almost as much about history and stuff as my tutor. Like my parents always told me, you can't judge a book by its cover."

"I think I remember your dad saying that a few times," Sam said thoughtfully as one of the restaurant employees set a pair of delicious-looking sandwiches on the table in front of them.

"Really?" Star felt her heart jump. "It's so cool that you remember them. I hardly ever get to talk about them with anyone who actually knew them. I mean, of course I still talk about them with Missy and Nans . . ."

"Nans!" Sam cried. "Oh, she was always my favorite. Does she still have that orange cat? What was his name— Mr. Wellington?"

"No, he died a few years ago. He was about a hundred years old even when I was a baby." Star shook her head, still amazed that Sam recalled so much about Star and her life, while Star didn't remember anything about the other girl at all. "So how long were we friends, anyway?" she asked, determined to jog her own memory. "You live here in Europe now, right? When did that happen?"

Sam took a sip of her water before answering. "My mom's a college professor," she said. "She teaches European history, and she finished her Ph.D. around the time you and I were in kindergarten together. She was looking for a job at one of the local universities, but wound up getting some totally amazing offer to come teach in Switzerland. My dad is a graphic designer, which means he can work pretty much anywhere, and so they decided she would take the job." She shrugged. "I guess they thought they'd just come over to Europe for a few years and then go back to the U.S., but they ended up loving it here. I remember I told you I was moving while we were sitting on that old swing set in your backyard. Missy was there too, and that kid Aaron Bickford—"

Star felt herself blush at the mention of the latter name. She and Aaron had known each other forever, though it was only in the past couple of years that they'd started to look at each other as more than friends. Star's career had exploded at just about that time, so they hadn't really had a chance to figure out exactly how they felt about each other. But during a recent trip to visit Star on tour, Aaron had given Star her very first real kiss. Ever since, even thinking about him made Star's heart beat a little faster.

"Really?" Star said, pushing all thoughts of Aaron aside for the moment. "I—I remember that swing set. Dad took it down when I was in second grade because he was afraid it would fall apart."

She felt terrible for not remembering the moment, which seemed to have been important to Sam. *Star* seemed to have been important to Sam—it was obvious that she remembered their friendship fondly. So why didn't Star remember it at all?

"What's the matter?" Sam asked, peering at her. "You look kind of bummed or something."

"I'm sorry," Star blurted. "I just feel mega guilty for not remembering any of this. I guess you were a better friend to me than I was to you."

Sam laughed. "Don't spaz about it," she reassured Star. "I know you had tons of friends back then—you were, like, the most popular kid in town! Even the older kids liked to hang out with you." She shrugged. "Besides, I've changed a lot since then. My hair used to be blonde and sort of wavy when I was younger; it's a lot darker and straighter now. And it *was* a long time ago. I hadn't really thought about you in a while when you got famous. Seeing you on PopTV every other second reminded me pretty fast, though." She laughed.

That made Star feel a little better, though she still wished she could remember the things Sam was describing. She hated to think that being famous meant she might forget about people who'd once been important to her.

Still, Sam is right, she told herself, covering her consternation by taking a bite of her sandwich and chewing it carefully. *I really did have a lot of friends back then—Dad used to joke that I liked to invite the entire state of Pennsylvania over to play in our backyard. So what if I don't remember her specifically, especially if we only knew each other for a short time? The important thing is that we've found each other again, so we have a chance to pick up our friendship where we left off.*

"So tell me more," she said eagerly, leaning forward to gaze at Sam hopefully. "What have you been doing since you moved to Europe? It must be really cool to live here full-time."

Sam waved one hand lazily. "Eh," she said. "It's not really that different from America, really. Anyway, I want to hear more about you—like how the search for your parents is going. I couldn't believe it when I heard they disappeared like that!"

"I know. My baby brother, too. You didn't know him—he was born way after you moved away. He was only two when they disappeared." Star swallowed hard, thinking about how much she missed her family.

"Sorry," Sam said, looking worried. "I didn't mean to make you feel bad by talking about this."

Star forced a smile to her face. "No, no!" she cried. "It's okay. I love talking about my family, especially with people who know them. It makes me miss them a little less, you know?"

"I know," Sam said softly. "It was sort of the same way for

me after we moved. I missed Pennsylvania so much—the only thing that kept me from going crazy was talking on the phone to my grandparents."

"Your grandparents?" Star asked. "Do they still live in New Limpet?"

"No," Sam replied, her face twisting into a slight grimace. "They're not from there. They live in another part of the state."

"Oh." Noticing that Sam looked upset and guessing that she missed her grandparents a lot, Star decided to change the subject. "So your mom's a professor, huh?" she said lightly. "Does she know anything about Napoleon? Because my tutor keeps threatening to give me a quiz, and I still haven't made it halfway through the chapter in my history book."

Sam looked surprised. "You mean you have to do schoolwork?" she said. "But you're, like, a superstar. What do you care about Napoleon and stuff?"

Star shrugged. It wasn't the first time someone had expressed surprise at that very same topic. In fact, she'd been thinking about writing a little article about her studies with Mags for the Star Power Web site—if she ever found the time.

"I want to go to college someday," she told Sam. "That means I need to learn stuff now so I'm ready. Besides, my parents think education is super important, and I know they'd be disappointed if I slacked off just because I'm famous or whatever."

"Oh, right!" Sam said quickly. "I remember that. Your parents always talked about how school was important. Even in kindergarten. So what's your tutor like?"

"Mrs. Nattle is great." Star smiled fondly as she thought about Mags. "She's really cool about working my school stuff in around all the other things I have to do. And she tries to make things interesting—like now that we're in Europe, she's having me focus mostly on European history and geography and stuff like that. Last week when we were in Germany, she took me to see what's left of the Berlin Wall and we learned all about it. It was cool to be right there where it all happened, you know?"

Sam nodded. "We went to Berlin on vacation last year," she said. "Mom was giving a lecture there. Come to think of it, it had something to do with Napoleon." She rolled her eyes. "Mom is big on Napoleon. I've been hearing all about him since I was in diapers."

"Really? Maybe you can fill me in." Star giggled. "Otherwise I'll probably flunk my quiz, and Mrs. Nattle will tell Mike, and he'll skin me alive."

"Mike?" Sam asked curiously, reaching for a pot of brown mustard on the next table.

"Mike Mosley. He's my manager," Star said. "He's been in charge of my career since the very beginning."

Sam looked interested. "Really? How did you first meet him?" she asked. "I mean, did you, like, go try out somehow, or did he spot you singing somewhere and come up to you, or what?"

Star leaned back in her chair. She was having such a nice time talking with Sam that she'd nearly finished her sandwich without realizing it. "He heard about me from a friend of a friend after I won this local talent show," she said. "He called and asked Mom and Dad if I would sing for him. When we first met, I was a little scared of him—he's like six and a half feet tall, with this big bushy mustache and cowboy boots. But then he smiled, and I could totally tell he was just a big mush underneath his gruff outsides. After that, the rest is history."

"Wow," Sam said. "So it sounds like that talent show was sort of your big break, huh?"

"I guess. I used to beg my parents to let me enter stuff like that. I always loved to sing, and I thought performing for people was the most fun thing ever. . . ."

The two girls continued to talk, one topic sliding easily into another. Star couldn't help noticing that the conversation returned frequently to the subject of her career, but Star didn't really mind. She couldn't blame Sam for being curious about the daily life of a celebrity; if their positions had been switched, Star was sure she'd be the same way. Besides, she didn't really care that much what they talked about. It was nice to spend time with someone her own age—someone who wasn't asking for her autograph or treating her like some kind of alien life form visiting from Planet Superstar. She'd missed just hanging out like that with friends ever since Missy and the others had left after their recent visit.

Finally, out of the corner of her eye, she saw Tank glance at his watch, fold his paper, and stand up. He walked over and cleared his throat.

"Oh no, Tank," Star exclaimed. "Is it time to go already?"

"'Fraid so," Tank said. "Sorry, girls."

"Can't she stay just a few more minutes?" Sam wheedled. "Please?"

Tank shook his head. "Sorry," he said again, his voice sympathetic. "She's got appointments, and if we're late, Mosley will have my head."

"It's okay," Star told Sam, swallowing back her own disappointment. She wished that for once she could change her schedule just because she felt like it. But she knew better—if she tried to blow off her afternoon appointments, it would only mean more work and hassle for Mike and the rest of her team. "We can get together again before I leave Switzerland, okay?"

They thanked the restaurant people and headed for the front door. Tank was in the lead, and when he peered out the windows, he shook his head in annoyance. "Looks like they tracked us down here after all," he said, pulling out his cell phone.

Star peered around him and saw a crowd gathered on the sidewalk just outside. She sighed.

"Sorry about this," she told Sam. "We'll have to wait here until Tank gets some backup."

Sam's eyes were wide as she stared at the throngs outside. One of the photographers pressed his camera to the shop window and started taking pictures.

"This is so cool!" Sam exclaimed. "Do people really do this everywhere you go?"

"You have no idea," Star replied. "It's kind of fun sometimes, but more often it's a hassle." She shrugged. "I mean, it's cool that my fans want to see me. But the reporters can be awfully pushy sometimes, and it would be nice to be able to walk around outside like a normal person without worrying about getting trampled, you know?"

Sam was still staring out the window. "I guess," she said, sounding unconvinced. "But just think—all those people out there are screaming for you! How cool is that?"

Star grinned, realizing she had once thought of it the exact same way. The first time she'd emerged from her limo to a waiting crowd of screaming fans, she'd almost fainted from excitement. Now, seeing it through Sam's eyes, some of that feeling came back to her.

"I guess it's pretty cool," she admitted, impulsively putting an arm around Sam's shoulder and squeezing her into a hug.

Five

The next day Star returned to the hotel suite after another busy morning of appointments. "Hi," she greeted Lola, who was sitting at the saloon bar hand-sewing some sparkles onto one of Star's stage outfits. "Is Mrs. Nattle here?"

"Not right now," Lola mumbled around the pins she was holding between her teeth. "Mags went out to run some errands. Should be back in a couple of hours. Tank's out too—took that dog of yours for a walk. Why?"

Star shrugged. "One of my interviews got postponed, so I have a few free hours before I have to start getting ready for tonight's show. I thought I could use it to sit down with Mrs. Nattle and go over that Napoleon chapter I've been reading in my history book. A few parts are kind of hard to understand, and I want to be ready for that quiz she keeps threatening."

Lola looked sympathetic. "Wish I could help you out myself, babydoll," she said apologetically. "But history was my worst subject back in school. My teachers always said I must've thought my own appearance in the world was the most interesting bit of history ever, because I was completely hopeless with anything that took place before I was born."

Star giggled. "That's okay," she said. "Maybe Tank can help me out for a while when he gets back. Oh! Or, I have a better idea . . ."

She hurried toward the phone at the end of the bar. Dialing the front desk, she asked the operator to help her locate a local number.

"The last name is Bradley," she said.

Moments later she was connected. Sam herself answered the phone.

"Star!" she cried, sounding surprised and thrilled. "Hey, what's up?"

"I have a favor to ask you," Star replied. "You said you know all about Napoleon, right? Well, how about coming over here to help me study for a while? I can order us some room service, and it'll be almost like a little party or something."

"Awesome!" Even through the phone, Sam's voice sounded excited. "I'll be right there!"

Less than half an hour later Star was peering through the peephole at Sam standing in the hallway outside. On Lola's advice, she'd called Mike on his cell phone to let him know about her impulsive invitation. Mike had sounded slightly disapproving, but he agreed that it was a good idea for Star to get some help with her history homework.

"Hey!" Star greeted Sam happily, swinging open the door. "Thanks a zillion for coming at such short notice. Come on in."

"Whoa, check this place out!" Sam stepped inside and immediately turned on her heel, surveying the Wild West suite's main room. "I read about this hotel in the newspaper when it opened last year, but I've never been inside before. It's even more outrageous on the inside than on the outside!"

Star giggled. "I know. It's totally over the top, isn't it?" she said. "It's the coolest hotel I've ever stayed in."

"Is that real?" Sam took a step toward the mechanical bull. "Have you tried it out yet?"

"Not yet, but I totally want to." Star stepped over and patted the mechanical bull. As she backed away, she almost tripped over some boxes and shopping bags stacked at the edge of the platform. "Hey, what's all this stuff?" she called to Lola, who was still sitting at the counter working on her costumes.

Lola looked up. "Oh, I forgot to tell you, babydoll," she said. "Tricia dropped off that stuff while you were out earlier.

I haven't had a chance to go through it yet."

"But what is it?" Sam asked, staring curiously at a glittery bit of fabric sticking out of one of the bags.

Star shrugged. "If Tricia brought it, it's probably just more freebie stuff," she said. Noticing Sam's confused look, she went on. "A lot of designers and different companies or whatever like to send their stuff over. They're hoping I'll wear it in public, or better yet onstage or in an interview or something. That way the product gets free publicity." She flipped open the top of one of the boxes and grabbed a pair of purple-swirled sunglasses with pink mirrored lenses. "Like these, see? If my fans see me wearing these, some of them might want to go out and get a pair for themselves. Get it?"

"Crazy," Sam murmured, leaning over to look into the open box.

Star laughed, suddenly feeling slightly uncomfortable. She hoped Sam didn't think she was bragging.

"I know it's nuts," she said. "It doesn't make any sense to me at all. The first few times it happened, I kept wanting to write thank-you notes to the people who sent it." She grinned. "Mike had to keep talking me out of it."

Sam shook her head. "No, I don't mean crazy bad," she said. "I mean crazy wild! How cool is it to get all this free stuff? See, this is the stuff us ordinary people don't even know about being a superstar."

"I guess," Star agreed, relieved that Sam didn't think she was trying to show off. "So are you hungry? I didn't want to order food without you. We could call room service now, or wait until after we do some studying. What do you think?"

"Huh?" Sam glanced up. "Oh, right. Studying." She bit her lip. "But aren't you going to look through this stuff first?"

Star blinked, staring down at the boxes. After the first few times, pawing through the freebies had lost some of its appeal. When she had enough free time, she still sometimes looked through for things she wanted to keep or send to Missy or Nans or other people she knew. Otherwise she let Lola sort through it for her.

"Oh," she said. "Um, I guess we could check it out before we get started."

She could tell the other girl was itching to see what was in the boxes. To Sam, getting free stuff probably seemed just as cool and exciting as it had to Star herself at first. Besides, it seemed a little unfair to demand that her new friend help her with her schoolwork without offering any fun in return.

"Are you sure?" Sam asked eagerly. "I mean, if it's really okay . . ."

"Go for it." Star giggled, enjoying the sudden flash of excitement that lit up Sam's brown eyes. "Maybe there's some stuff that will fit you in there—we look like we probably wear about the same size."

For the next few minutes the girls dug through the boxes and bags. They found several other pairs of sunglasses, each trendier-looking than the last. The boxes also held all sorts of costume jewelry, beauty products, and even a set of scented candles.

"How do they expect you to give extra publicity to these?" Sam asked, looking perplexed as she held a candle in each hand. "I mean, unless you decide to wear them as earrings or something . . ."

Star laughed. "I don't know," she admitted.

Just then the suite's main door opened and Tank stepped in with Dudley at his heels. "We're back," Tank announced as he leaned over to unsnap the little dog's leash.

"Finally!" Star exclaimed. "That was some long walk."

Tank grinned at her. "Hey, Zurich's an interesting place," he said. "Dudley and I wanted to see the sights. And chase the swans in the river." He shrugged his massive shoulders. "Well, okay, maybe that last part was just Dudley."

Star laughed. Dudley was one of the friendliest dogs she'd

ever known. He loved every person he met and would never think of chasing a cat or growling at another dog. The one exception to his good nature was that he nursed an intense—though clumsy—killer instinct when it came to birds of any kind.

Dudley bounded over to slurp Star's outstretched hand with his pink tongue. "Silly boy," Star told him. "Don't you realize swans are bigger than you? You don't want to mess with them."

Dudley let out a happy bark, his curly tail wagging furiously. Giving Star one last lick, he turned to sniff curiously at Sam.

"Hello, little guy," Sam cooed. "He's so cute! Is he yours, Star?"

Star nodded. "This is Dudley Do-Wrong," she told the other girl. "Mom and Dad got him for me just before my little brother, Timmy, was born. He's been my best bud ever since." She grabbed the pug and gave him a quick squeeze.

As Tank and Lola wandered into the kitchen and Dudley settled down on the padded floor near the mechanical bull for a nap, Star and Sam returned to their previous activity. The boxes and bags of gifts seemed never to end. They found more jewelry, more beauty products, more of everything.

One bag even held a gift basket of dog toys, which Star unwrapped and tossed to Dudley. He woke up just long enough to sink his teeth into a plush chicken before going back to sleep.

But most of all the girls found clothes—shoes, hats, belts, skirts, scarves, tank tops, socks, pants, and more. Style-wise the items ranged from teddy bear–print pajamas suitable for a toddler to hip-looking jeans and T-shirts to a large jewel-studded leather bustier.

"Whoa, check this out!" Sam said with a giggle, holding up the bustier. "I think both of us could fit into this!"

Lola had just returned from the kitchen holding a cup of tea. She immediately set down her drink, hurried over, and snatched the bustier away from them.

"Sorry, girls. Not for fourteen-year-olds," she said firmly. "It's much more suited to an old lady like me." She stepped around the bar to the mirrored wall behind it, holding the item up against herself before disappearing into one of the bedrooms.

The girls returned to their search. "Ooh! Check this out," Sam said, pulling a satiny blue-green jacket from beneath several pairs of shoes. "I love this color."

"Try it on," Star suggested.

Sam smiled uncertainly. "Are you sure? It looks super expensive . . ."

Star laughed. "Yeah, but so what? You're shopping at the free store, remember? Go ahead, see if it fits."

Sam tentatively slid her arms into the jacket's sleeves. "It fits!" she said shyly.

"Cool," Star said. "Then it's yours."

"Really?" Sam's eyes widened hopefully. "Are you for real? I can keep it?"

"For real," Star assured her with a smile. One of her favorite parts about her life as a celebrity was being able to do nice things for her friends. Star had always been gener-ous, and it felt great to share her good fortune with others.

"Thanks, Star!" Sam rushed over to the saloon mirror. "Wow!" she said, turning this way and that to examine her reflection. "With this jacket on, I look like I'm almost ready to hit the stage at the Notey Awards show or something."

Star followed, looking over Sam's shoulder. "It looks great," she agreed. "There's just one problem—you definitely need to upgrade the rest of your outfit to match."

Sam giggled. "Let's go!"

Soon Sam had exchanged her jeans and lavender sweater

for a black minidress, wild-patterned tights, and the blue-green jacket. The purple mirrored sunglasses, perched on the end of her nose, finished off the outfit.

"How do I look?" she asked, striking a pose with one elbow on the mechanical bull. "Do I look like a real superstar?"

Star grinned. "Totally. I'm sure PopTV will be calling any second."

By that time both girls were hungry. Leaving the freebie boxes, they called room service and ordered lunch. Sam couldn't decide between the all-American burger and the California avocado salad, so Star insisted she order both.

"Tank will clean up whatever's left over," she said. "He's a bottomless pit when it comes to food."

It seemed pointless to break out the books in the short time before the food arrived, so instead Star showed Sam the rest of the two adjoining suites. After that, at Sam's urging, Star finally took her long-delayed ride on the mechanical bull. However, it only lasted about a second and a half before she found herself flying off onto the padded floor.

"Okay, that wasn't as much fun as I thought it would be," she joked as she climbed to her feet.

Sam giggled. "How could you tell?" she teased playfully.

"I barely had time to blink before you were off."

"Oh yeah?" Star retorted in mock anger. "Let's see you do any better!"

Soon Sam was sitting atop the mechanical bull's rounded form, one hand tucked into the handle at the front. She raised her free arm like a real cowboy. "Let 'er rip!" she called.

Star flipped the switch on the control panel. The bull wheezed into action, bucking and spinning faster and faster. Sam held on, her body moving gracefully with the machine's flips and turns. Finally Star turned off the switch.

"That was fun," Sam said with a giggle as the mechanical bull came to a stop.

"How did you do that?" Star exclaimed. "I mean, I thought I was in pretty good shape from dancing and stuff. But that was hard!"

Sam swung down off the machine. "I've taken horseback riding lessons since I was six. Guess they came in handy."

Star smiled weakly, feeling a jolt in the pit of her stomach as Sam's comment reminded her of Missy's e-mail. But she did her best to hide her consternation from the other girl, not wanting to take away from the fun mood.

Luckily the food arrived at that moment, wheeled into the room by a server dressed in a hoop skirt and bonnet straight out of *Gone with the Wind*. By the time the food was set up and the girls settled down to eat, Star had pushed her worries about Missy to the back of her mind.

As they ate, the conversation turned to the subject of Star's family. "So what's your little brother like?" Sam asked as she scooped a chunk of avocado into her mouth. "Does he look like you?"

Sam smiled, grateful to hear Sam use the present tense. Too many people referred to her family as if they were gone for good.

"His hair is darker than mine already," she replied. "I think he's going to grow up to look like Dad." Suddenly she had an idea. "Oh! But here, I can show you! I'll be right back."

She rushed to her bedroom. A moment later she returned holding a framed photo in one hand and a large photo album tucked under the other arm.

"This is my favorite picture of all of us," she said, handing the picture to Sam. "See? That's Timmy right there. But we were at the beach, so he was wearing a sun bonnet and you can't really see his hair. But there are some other pictures in here."

She set the photo album on the table and flipped through it, looking for a clearer picture of her brother. Sam watched curiously. "Hey, who's that?" she asked, pointing to a photo on one of the pages.

Star paused. "That? It's me and Mike," she said.

"No, I mean that other guy, there." Sam sounded excited. "Isn't that Kynan from Boysterous?"

"Oh, yeah." Star stared down at the photo. "Someone took that at an awards show last year. Ky is a really nice guy; I've met him a few times. But I stuck it in here because it's one of my favorite pictures of Mike. This album mostly has friends and family in it." She flipped the page. "Hey, I have some old pictures from elementary school in here—I wonder if you're in any of them."

"So don't you have any more photos of you with other celebrities and stuff?" Sam asked.

Star shrugged. "Oh, sure," she said. "I've got whole books full of clippings and photos. But those are separate." Suddenly noticing the eager look on Sam's face, she added, "Er, would you like to see some of those, too?"

"I'd love to!" Sam exclaimed.

Soon they were flipping through one of Star's other albums, the remains of their lunch forgotten. This one was crammed full of publicity shots and candids of Star standing with various other famous faces—other singers and musicians, TV and film actors, politicians, athletes, producers, and socialites. Sam seemed more and more fascinated with each page. Star obligingly told her the story behind each shot, even though they didn't seem very interesting to her. Most of the celebrities were people she'd met in passing at awards shows, movie premieres, or other industry functions.

But it probably all seems way cool and exotic to Sam, she reminded herself. In fact, Star had to admit that she still got excited at such meetings sometimes. For instance, she had been thrilled to meet Eddie Urbane for the first time just before the start of her tour—at least until she'd figured out that he was self-centered and egotistical.

As they reached the end of the album, the door between the two suites opened and Mike walked in. "Howdy, girls," he greeted Star and Sam, sounding distracted. "Hate to interrupt. But Star, I need to check in with you about adding somethin' to your schedule."

"What's that, Mike?" Star asked in surprise. Mike usually handled her schedule on his own.

"Just worked out a deal with the Zoom Juice people," he said. "They were interested in signing you to do some ads for them, remember?"

Star nodded. Mike and Tricia had mentioned that the

makers of a popular sports drink wanted Star to appear in their new TV commercials. Mike had explained that in addition to the money the ads would earn her, the extra exposure would help to sell more albums and concert tickets.

"Well, they're all het up about gettin' started right away," Mike went on. "I tried to explain that you're busy as a dog at a cat show right now, but they really want the ads to start runnin' by Labor Day weekend." He sighed. "So I hate to ask you this, but how'd you feel about givin' up a day or two of your break to do some shootin' in New York?"

Star swallowed hard, one hand wandering up to touch her star necklace. Then she nodded. "Sure," she said. "That sounds okay. Tell them I'll do it."

Mike's face broke into a smile. "Thanks, sweetheart," he said. "I'll go call them back now."

When he left the room, Star let out the sigh she'd been holding in. Sam glanced at her.

"What's the matter?" she asked. "Aren't you psyched about doing ads for Zoom Juice? I love that stuff! I just wish they had all the flavors over here in Europe."

"I love it too," Star said. "It's not that." She bit her lip, wondering if she should say what she was thinking. Then she shrugged. Sam was her friend, right? That meant she could be honest with her. "I just wish I didn't have to do it during my break. I was really looking forward to having some time at home to just chill and be a normal girl for a change."

"Bummer. But at least you know the ad will be cool," Sam said, sounding a little distracted. "Remember that awesome one Eddie Urbane did a year or two ago? That old singer Athena Quincy did one too, and she hardly ever does commercials. And . . ."

Sam rambled on, listing more celebrities who'd appeared in Zoom Juice ads. Suddenly she cut herself off.

"Oops, sorry," she said, reaching across the table for Star's hand and giving it a squeeze. "I'm babbling, aren't I? Sorry. You're totally right—it stinks that you have to give up part of your vacation."

"Thanks." Star smiled. Sam's sympathy actually made her feel a tiny bit better. "But it's not really a big deal. I just really feel like I need some time to reconnect with my f-friends." Her voice caught slightly on the last word as Missy's e-mail flew back into her mind.

Sam peered at her with concern. "Hey, what's up?" she said. "You look majorly upset now."

Star sighed. "It's nothing," she said. "Really, it's not, I'm just being silly. It's just that I got this e-mail from Missy, and . . ."

Without quite realizing it, the whole story poured out. Sam listened sympathetically, not saying a word, as Star described Missy's e-mail and her own reaction to it.

". . . so it's not like Missy did anything wrong," Star finished. "Not even a little bit. I don't even know why I feel so weird about it all." She sighed. "I guess it just reminded me how different my life is now than it used to be. And that I can't really go back even if I wanted to. Or something like that."

Sam stood up and hurried around the table, almost tripping over Dudley, who was sniffing for crumbs on the floor. She reached down and gave Star a big hug.

"It's okay," she said. "Don't be upset, Star. I don't blame you for feeling weird." She straightened up. "Hey, I have an idea! How about if we go riding over here? That way, it'll be sort of like you're still doing the same stuff as Missy. Maybe it'll make you feel better about the whole thing."

Star wasn't sure that would work, but she was touched by Sam's obvious concern. "Sure," she said. "Do you think we could find a place to do it? It would have to be somewhere sort of private so we wouldn't get mobbed."

"The stable where I take lessons would be perfect," Sam declared. "It's totally private. I know they'd be happy to let us go on a nice trail ride whenever you want."

The other girl's enthusiasm was catching. "I'll talk to Mike," Star promised. "If he thinks it's okay, I'll have him set it up. Okay?" She smiled at Sam. "And thanks."

Sam shrugged. "Hey, what are friends for?"

Star sighed happily. Sam might not be Missy, but she was starting to feel like a true friend.

"Okay, enough of my whining and complaining," Star said briskly, pushing back from the table. "We still have time to do a little studying before I have to get ready for my concert tonight. So let's get started!"

Six

"Did you get the tickets?" Star asked into the phone.

She was sitting at the bar in the "saloon" in her bathrobe. Lola had makeup, hair gel, and other supplies spread out on the bar as she began preparing Star's hair and face for that night's show. While she always did most of the finishing work in the dressing room at the concert venue, the stylist liked to get a head start at the hotel whenever possible.

"Uh-huh," Sam's voice replied in Star's ear. "Thanks! The messenger just left."

Star smiled. She'd asked Mike to send a pair of front-row tickets and backstage passes for her concert over to Sam's home. "Good," she said. "And you're totally welcome. Thanks again for helping me study earlier."

"Too bad we didn't have time to do that much," Sam replied, sounding a bit sheepish. "I didn't realize how much time we were spending hanging out and eating and stuff."

"That's okay," Star replied, shifting the phone to her other ear as Lola moved from one side of her face to the other. "So, is your brother going to take you to the concert?"

"Yup." Sam giggled. "He acts like he's doing me a huge favor, but I think he's actually almost as excited as I am to be going. Typical seventeen-year-old boy!"

"How are you guys getting to the show? Does your brother have a car?" Star asked.

"No, but my dad said we can use his."

Noticing Mike wandering through the room, Star asked Sam to hold on for a second and then put her hand over the phone's mouthpiece. "Psst, Mike," she said, waving him over. "I think I'll see if Sam and her brother want to ride over with us tonight. Is that okay?"

Mike stopped short. "No," he said. "It's not okay."

"What?" Star was surprised. "Why not?"

"You don't need any distractions right before a big show," her manager replied firmly. "And Samantha is nothin' if not distracting. I'm sure she can find her way to the stadium herself."

Star opened her mouth to argue. Then she shut it again, realizing that Mike had a point. Still, she couldn't help being disappointed.

"Sam?" she said, uncovering the mouthpiece.

"Did I hear what I think I heard?" Sam burbled excitedly. "Do we really get to ride to the concert in your limo?"

Star gulped, realizing she should have pressed the mute button rather than rely on her hand to muffle her voice. "Sorry," she said. "I just asked. But Mike didn't think it would work out. I'm really, really sorry."

"Oh." Sam sounded crestfallen. "Oh well," she added more brightly. "That's okay, no biggie. I know you celebrities need special quiet time to prepare and stuff. A car ride isn't just a car ride for you, you know? I totally understand."

Star bit her lip. Sam's comment made it sound as if she thought that all celebrities were exotic, sensitive creatures with needs much different from those of ordinary people. Star always wished there was an easy way to explain that it just wasn't true—celebrities *were* ordinary people just like everyone else.

"Hey, I have an idea of how to make it up to you," she said quickly into the phone. "How about if you ride back with us *after* the concert instead?" She glanced over at Mike, who was still listening. He rolled his eyes, then nodded. "Mike said that would be okay."

"Cool!" Sam sounded thrilled. "Thanks, Star! I can't wait."

90

"Thank you! You guys are awesome!" Star shouted breathlessly. Her audience screamed louder than ever, jumping up and down. Their frantically waving arms and the bobbing and swaying of their countless homemade signs made the entire stadium look like a churning ocean of people.

Star glanced over her shoulder. She'd just finished singing a song called "Bright New Day," and her background dancers were scrambling to take their new positions on the darkened stage. Next in the show was a musical break, when the band played a long instrumental introduction to one of the hits from Star's first album. That would give her enough time for a costume change before she had to be back onstage to sing the opening lines of the song.

Until the dancers were ready, Star was supposed to distract the audience for a moment or two. She skipped to the front of the stage, causing the fans in the first few rows to surge forward. Luckily a line of security guards was ready to hold them back.

Star peered over the footlights, trying to see into the first row. She hadn't seen Sam yet, but she assumed she was out there somewhere.

I hope she's having fun, Star thought. *I'm so glad she could come tonight!*

A second later she spotted Sam standing on her seat in the front row. She waved wildly, her mouth opening and closing. Star guessed that Sam was calling her name, though she couldn't hear her over the wild shrieks and yells of the crowd. Beside Sam was a teenage boy with brown hair the same color as Sam's.

Guess that's her older brother, Star thought.

She noticed that Sam was wearing the blue-green jacket Star had given her. Grinning at her friend, she shot her a thumbs-up before stepping back to talk to the crowd.

"I hope you guys are ready to see some awesome dancing now," she said, her amplified voice carrying over the din. "My dancers are the best in the business, and they worked up this number just for you. Enjoy!"

She bounded offstage as the band launched into the instrumental break. Seconds later she was ducking into the canvas quick-change booth set up just offstage, where Lola and her assistants were waiting to help her change into the next outfit. To Star's surprise, someone else was there, too.

"Erin?" she blurted, startled to see the dancer. "I thought you were out there right now." She gestured toward the stage with her chin, keeping her arms straight out to the sides as

Lola and an assistant rapidly unhooked the fasteners down the back of her dress.

"I was, until halfway through the last number," Erin said, rolling her eyes. "That's when my laces broke."

Star glanced down and saw that Erin was looping a set of thigh-high pink laces up her right leg. Nearby she saw a broken set of identical laces lying on the floor.

"Yikes," she said. "What happened?"

Erin shrugged. "Who knows?" she said. "Guess I didn't check them closely enough before the show. Anyway, I think I slipped out of line without anyone seeing. I'll just sneak back on when you make your next entrance—that way everybody will be looking at you and won't notice me."

Star nodded. "I think it's going well tonight," she told Lola, raising her arms so the stylist could slip a glittery tank top over her head. "Oh! And Sam is here—I spotted her in the front row just now."

"That's great, babydoll," Lola said calmly as her hands continued to work swiftly. "Sounds good from back here, as always."

"Sam?" Erin asked curiously. "Uh-oh. Don't tell me Aaron has competition!" She waggled her eyebrows playfully.

"That's *Samantha*," Star informed her, blushing slightly as always at Aaron's name. "She's this girl who contacted me here—I don't really remember her, but I guess we were friends back in kindergarten. She lives here in Zurich now, so she decided to get back in touch when she heard I was here, and I gave her tickets to tonight's show."

"Ah, I see," Erin said with a grin. "So she's a groupie with an extra-creative story, huh?"

Star couldn't react to the dancer's statement—she was trying to keep her face perfectly still as Lola touched up her makeup. Besides, she could tell that Erin was just joking. Both Maxwell twins had a lively sense of humor, which was one of the things Star liked best about them.

But she couldn't help feeling a twinge of annoyance at the comment. Why did everyone seem to assume that Sam was up to no good? First Mike, and now Erin . . .

It doesn't matter, she told herself, banishing such negative thoughts from her mind as Lola put the finishing touches on her makeup. *I know that Sam's a true friend. And that's really all that matters.*

"This is so cool," Sam exclaimed as she watched Lola carefully pluck off the glittery stars she'd glued to Star's face and arms as part of her last costume. The concert had ended a few minutes earlier, and Star had invited Sam back to her dressing room.

Star giggled. "How many times are you going to say that?" she teased.

Sam stuck out her tongue. "Fine," she said, pretending to pout. "You might be all bored and jaded by your own fame and fabulousness, but you could at least let me enjoy it."

Lola had finished with the stars and was efficiently wiping off Star's lipstick with a tissue, so Star couldn't respond for a moment. It was fun seeing her own life through Sam's eyes, and Star was glad she'd invited the other girl to ride back to the hotel in the limo.

"It's too bad your brother couldn't come backstage and hang with us," Star commented when Lola moved on to her eye makeup, allowing her to speak again.

Sam shrugged. "He's a big dork anyway," she said. "Besides, he figured it would take a while to get out of the parking lot and stuff. So he's just going to meet me back at your hotel."

Just then Mike hurried into the room, his cell phone pressed to his ear. "Okay," he was saying. "Last I heard Lukas is still swearing it'll be done in plenty of time. I'm sure we'll all be sweatin' like a frog at a French picnic until we see the tape, though. All right. Talk to you tomorrow."

He hung up and glanced at Star. Lola had finished removing the stage makeup and was fluffing up Star's hair.

"Ready to roll?" Mike asked. Noticing Sam sitting at the makeup counter beside Star, he nodded to her. "Called that stable of yours, Miss Samantha," he said. "Y'all are signed up for a private trail ride tomorrow morning. All you have to do now is convince Tank to go with you."

Tank entered the room just in time to hear. "Trail ride?" he said. "I'm there. I love riding—used to do it all the time when I lived in South America."

Star stared at him. She hadn't known that Tank had ever lived in South America, let alone that he rode horses there. But that was really no surprise—she'd always guessed that if Tank ever decided to tell them his complete life story, it would take him about a week.

Soon the whole group was heading for the back entrance. Tank paused at the door. "There's quite a crowd out there, as usual," he warned. "Star, did you warn your friend about what to do?"

"Yup," Star confirmed. She glanced over at Sam. "Remember, just keep moving slowly forward with the group. Don't say anything, just smile or keep a neutral expression. And try not to make eye contact with the reporters."

Mike nodded. "And don't take this the wrong way, kiddo," he told Sam kindly. "But try to keep a few steps behind Star. She's the one the photographers want—if you block their view, even accidentally, they can get kinda mean."

Star giggled. "Right," she said. "Leave that to Tank—he likes it when they're mean to him. It gives him an excuse to cuss them out in Portuguese or Swahili or something."

Tank grinned at her. Then he turned and flung open the door, leading the way down the set of concrete steps and onto the sidewalk.

Star pasted a smile on her face and stepped after him, waving to the crowd she couldn't quite see thanks to the blinding camera flashes going off all around her. She was vaguely aware of Sam walking down the steps behind her.

"Star! Star! Over here!"

As usual, reporters clamored for her attention. She glanced one way and then the other, still smiling and waving.

"Coming through," Tank growled.

A tall, lanky photographer leaned forward over the guard ropes. "Hey Star!" he yelled in an Australian accent. "Over here!"

When Star obligingly turned and smiled in his direction, he snapped a few quick pictures. Before she could turn away, he called out to her again.

"Star! Who's your young friend there?"

Star blinked, realizing he had to be talking about Sam. She kept moving, not planning to answer. She almost jumped out of her skin when she felt someone suddenly grab her around the shoulders.

"I'm her good friend Sam!" Sam shouted, squeezing Star tight. "Sam Bradley! Hello, Zurich!" With the arm that wasn't clutching Star, she waved enthusiastically to the crowd and added a few words in German.

With that, all sorts of reporters shouted out their own questions about Sam's identity. Star had to stop herself from rolling her eyes. She still found it completely bizarre that even the most boringly ordinary parts of her life seemed so interesting to so many people. *Since when did a fourteen-year-old hanging out with a pal her own age become international news?* she wondered, biting back a sigh.

"We're old friends!" Sam shouted before Star could do anything to stop her. "And you'd better keep an eye out for me—someday I'll be as famous as my friend Star!"

Mike lunged forward. "All right," he said grimly. "That'll be enough of that."

With Tank's help, he hustled the girls along to the limo. After giving one last wave to the crowd, Star ducked inside. She turned to face Sam as she climbed in after her.

"What was all that?" Star asked.

Sam's face was flushed and her brown eyes sparkled with excitement. "Sorry about that," she said breathlessly. "I know you told me to keep quiet. But I just couldn't help it! I hope you're not mad."

Star sighed, her annoyance fading immediately. "Of course not." She smiled at the other girl sympathetically.

Of course Sam had gotten excited. Any normal person would when exposed to something like that. Star remembered how intense she had found such moments in the beginning.

Just because those sorts of crowds are an everyday nuisance to me now, I shouldn't expect everyone else to react the same way, she reminded herself.

She glanced at Sam, who was oohing and aahing over the limo's luxurious interior. Smiling at her friend's enthusiasm, Star settled back against the leather seat for the ride home.

☆ ☆ ☆ ☆ ☆

It was late by the time the gang got back to the hotel, said good night to Sam and her brother, and headed upstairs. Star was yawning as Tank opened the door to the Wild West suite.

"Whew, I'm beat," Star said, following him inside. "Think I'll head straight to bed. I don't want to be too tired for that trail ride tomorrow."

Mike put a hand on her shoulder. "Star, wait."

She glanced at him, surprised by his serious tone. "What?"

Mike sighed and rubbed his mustache, wandering farther into the room and sitting down on one of the saloon stools. Meanwhile Tank and the others melted away, leaving the two of them alone.

"Star," Mike began. "Didn't you think that stunt Sam pulled was—well, a tad odd?"

"What stunt?" For a second Star wasn't sure what her manager was talking about. "Oh, you mean talking to the reporters?" She shrugged, leaning against the bar. "You heard her in the car. She was just excited—having fun with the whole celebrity thing."

"Maybe." Mike sounded dubious. "I just wonder about her; that's all. I don't want you goin' around thinkin' she hung the moon if the truth is she's just usin' you."

Star frowned. Despite his rather convoluted phrasing, she suddenly understood exactly what Mike was saying—and she didn't like it.

"I appreciate your concern," she said, choosing her words carefully. "But you really don't have to worry. Sam is my friend—I know she is."

Mike shrugged. "I hope you're right, darlin'," he said, still sounding worried. "I really do."

Star couldn't stop thinking about Mike's comments as she climbed into bed a few minutes later. How could he still be so suspicious of Sam's motives? Why couldn't he just accept that she was who she claimed to be—a regular person enjoying a reunion with a old friend—without reading all sorts of dark and gloomy possibilities into the situation?

Well, it doesn't matter, she told herself, pulling the horseshoe-patterned down comforter up to her chin. *I trust Sam, and that's what matters. And I'm going to hang out with her as much as possible while we're here.*

Seven

"**This is so cool,**" Star said, taking a deep breath of the horse-and-leather-scented air.

Sam grinned at her. "Hey, that's my line," she joked.

Star tentatively reached a hand toward the pretty gray horse that was stretching its velvety nose toward her over a stall door. She was standing in a neatly swept stable aisle dressed in jeans, a T-shirt, and an old, scuffed pair of paddock boots borrowed from Sam. Nearby, Tank was chatting with the stable manager in German, while two other bodyguards kept a wary eye on their surroundings. Star knew that the guards were just doing their jobs, though she couldn't help thinking they could probably relax. Mike had arranged for privacy as usual, and aside from the horses and a couple of barn workers who had already asked for autographs and returned to tacking up or mucking stalls, the place was empty.

"So, which horse will I get to ride?" Star asked, feeling nervous and excited at the same time. She had been on horseback a few times before—mostly vacation trail rides, plus a few minutes riding bareback on the beach for one of the videos from her first album. But she didn't really know much about riding. "You guys won't, like, gallop off without me or anything, will you?"

"No way," Sam promised. "Come on, let's go find you a helmet to borrow."

Star followed the other girl down the barn aisle. As they passed the adults, Sam paused long enough to say a few words to the stable manager in German. Then she continued down the aisle, leading Star into a small room crammed with saddles, bridles, grooming tools, and all sorts of other items.

"It's so cool that you speak other languages," Star commented as Sam stepped toward a rack holding at least a dozen velvet or plastic riding helmets.

Sam shrugged. "You kind of have to, living here," she said. She grabbed a helmet off the rack and flipped it over to check the size. "I mean, I go to an American school, so our classes are mostly in English. And a lot of people in Europe speak English pretty well."

"I've noticed that," Star said with a nod.

"But you also hear a lot of the other languages just day to day," Sam went on. "You kind of pick it up whether you try to or not."

She set the helmet on Star's head, pushing it down until it fit snugly over her forehead. Then she nodded, looking pleased, and snapped the harness shut.

"That one should do," she said. "Hope it doesn't smush your hair down too much."

"Don't worry," Star assured her. "Lola can fix anything anyone does to my hair!"

The two girls hurried back out to the aisle. The barn workers were leading a pair of horses toward the entrance.

"That's Teufel." Sam pointed to the larger of the two horses, a rangy chestnut with two white stockings. "He's the one I usually ride in my lessons. Looks like they're putting you on Marzipan. You'll love him."

Star stared at the second horse, a short, rather pudgy bay gelding with kind eyes. She shivered with anticipation as the horse walked calmly past. "Okay, Marzipan. I hope you're as sweet as you look."

Soon they were mounted and riding across the stable yard. The stable manager was leading the trail on the gray horse Star had patted earlier, while Tank and one of the other bodyguards brought up the rear on a pair of large, sturdy warmbloods. Sam had explained that they would be exploring some of the miles of trails winding through the woods and parkland surrounding the stable.

At first all of Star's attention was focused on what she was doing. She felt herself stiffen nervously each time the horse's muscles moved beneath her, and the smooth leather reins felt awkward in her hands as she fumbled to hold them the way Sam had showed her. But no matter what she did, Marzipan walked calmly on beneath her, his tufted ears flicking back toward her once in a while as if he were checking on how she was doing. Eventually Star figured out how to manage the reins, and soon after that her body started to follow the easy, swinging rhythm of the horse's stride.

"Hey, this is sort of like dancing," she commented. "You can't think about anything else until you can catch the beat."

"Lookin' good, Star-baby," Tank called from behind her.

Star twisted around in the saddle and grinned at him. He looked as comfortable on his horse's back as he did behind the wheel of Star's tour bus. The other security guard also appeared to know what he was doing.

Guess I'm the only beginner in the group, Star thought, turning around again to face forward.

As they entered the woods on a wide, flat, well-kept trail, Sam rode her horse up beside Star's. "Are you having fun so far?" Sam asked, sounding slightly anxious.

"Definitely!" Star reached forward and gave her mount a pat on the neck. "Marzipan is totally taking care of me." She blinked as Sam's horse suddenly let out a loud snort and jumped forward a few steps.

"Quit it, Teufel!" Sam growled, quickly regaining control. She glanced at Star. "Teufel means 'devil' in German," she explained with a laugh. "They named him that for a reason."

Star nodded, impressed that her friend seemed so comfortable on the big, fiery gelding. Star was no chicken, but she wasn't sure she'd have the guts to climb atop a horse like Teufel—not unless she took a whole lot of riding lessons first.

And who knows when I'll get the chance to do that, she thought, her stomach clenching as she thought once again of Missy's note.

Soon she forgot about that as the whole group chatted about the horses, the pretty day, and the scenery they were passing. Eventually Tank and the stable manager started a lively discussion about European politics, slipping into mostly German as they rode side by side at the head of the group. The other security guard slipped to the back of the line and rode along quietly, humming to himself.

That left Star and Sam free to talk to each other. They

started out discussing their horses and other general subjects, but it wasn't long before the topic turned to Star's missing family.

"So, what else are the police doing to find them?" Sam asked. "I mean, you told me at lunch the other day about your trip to Florida—by the way, I still think it's totally cool that you actually got to fly in Eddie Urbane's private jet—but what's happening now?"

Star had told Sam all about a recent clue the police had found back in Florida. Mike had forbidden Star to leave the tour to fly back to the United States, but Eddie had offered to sneak her back to Florida in his plane. Star had been grateful to the other singer at first, though it hadn't taken long for her to realize that Eddie cared much more about the publicity he could gain from being seen with her than he did about helping her out. In the end the clue had turned out to be a hoax.

"Not much that I know about." Star glanced quickly at the two riders ahead of them, making sure that Tank wasn't listening. "Actually, though, I did hear something I wasn't supposed to," she added in a whisper. "Right after I got back from Florida, the detective who's handling the case over there called Mike to tell him they found another clue—a note in a bottle."

Sam's eyes widened with interest. "Really?" she asked. "So do they think it's from your parents?"

Star shrugged. "They're not sure, I guess," she said. "I mean, chances are it's probably just another hoax. But I'm sure Mike will tell me if anything comes of it."

"I don't know how you stand the suspense," Sam declared. "Especially since your parents are so totally cool and all. You must miss them like crazy."

"I do," Star said softly, leaning forward slightly as her horse stepped over a fallen branch in the trail. "Timmy, too. But I know they'll be back someday, so I just try to be patient."

Sam glanced over at her. "Sorry if talking about this is bumming you out," she said. "We can change the subject if you want."

"No!" Star said quickly. "I like talking about my family, but most people don't seem that comfortable talking about it with me—other than Missy, of course, but she's so far away . . ." She shrugged. "I mean, I can talk with Mike and the rest of my team too, but they didn't really know them—Mike met them before they disappeared, of course, but it's still not the same thing, you know?"

"Sure." Sam still looked slightly uncomfortable. "Okay,

then. What's the first thing you're going to do when your family comes back?"

Star had thought about that very question many times. "I'm not sure," she said dreamily. "Probably just hug them all within an inch of their lives, I guess. Tickle Timmy until he can hardly breathe, like I used to, and make Dad tell some of his corny old jokes. Oh! And I'm going to beg my mom to sing 'Star Bright' to me at least a million times—she used to sing me to sleep with it almost every night when I was little."

"'Star Bright'?" Sam repeated. "You mean that old Athena Quincy song?"

Star nodded. "That's where my name came from," she said. "It's my parents' favorite song—they danced to it at their wedding. I've always sort of toyed with the idea of recording it someday." She sighed, suddenly feeling slightly bashful. "But I'm not sure it's a good idea. I mean, everyone knows that song, and everyone knows Athena is like a total goddess of singing, you know? I don't want people to think I'm trying to imitate her or something."

"So what?" Sam shrugged. "If you love the song and it means something to you, you should go for it."

"But if people think it's nowhere near as good as the

original . . ." Star blushed slightly as she gave voice to the familiar thoughts.

"Who cares what people think? I'm sure your version will be great too!" Sam said loyally. "Anyway, you should go ahead and follow your dream, like your parents always told you."

Star shot her a quick, grateful glance. That did sound exactly like what her parents would say.

"You know, you may be right," she said, gathering up her reins as the trail opened up into a rolling meadow. "I think I'll talk to Mike about it soon. Now come on, let's ride!"

Star was still in a great mood when she, Sam, and Tank arrived back at the American. After their ride she and Sam had decided to top off the morning with a little shopping. Sam had already changed out of her riding clothes, and Star wanted to stop off back at the hotel to do the same.

When they entered the suite, Mike and Tricia were sitting at the bar working on a mailing, while Lola was busy cutting and pinning some silky star-patterned fabric she had draped over the mechanical bull. But the first thing Star focused on was Mags's stern face.

"There you are," the tutor said, tapping her foot. "I've been waiting for you. I hope you're ready for that Napoleon quiz, because today's the day."

Star gulped. All the excitement of hanging out with Sam, along with the usual chaos of being on tour, meant she'd barely made any progress on her studying. But she knew better than to offer up such excuses to Mags.

"I—I guess so, Mrs. Nattle," she said meekly.

"Good. I'll be right back with the test paper." Mags spun on her heel and hurried into the next suite.

Sam looked confused and slightly irritated. "But can't you do that later?" she asked. "I thought we were going shopping."

Lola glanced over at her with a grin. "Better not let Mags hear you talk like that, chickadee," she warned Sam playfully. "Or she just might make you take the test too!"

"Sorry," Star told Sam. "I have to do it now. Tank can drive you home if you want. If I don't do well on this quiz, I'll probably have to do some extra studying."

Sam shrugged. "That's okay," she said. "Maybe I can help out with whatever they're doing while you're taking your quiz." She gestured toward Mike and Tricia.

Mike looked surprised, but he shrugged agreeably. "Hey, if you're willing to lick envelopes, we'll take you up on it," he said. "Lord knows I don't want to sit here any longer than I have to."

"Cool." Sam pulled out a stool. "Just tell me what to do." She glanced over her shoulder at Star. "Then maybe we'll still have time for some shopping after you finish, right?"

Mags returned just in time to hear Sam's last comment. She glanced at the other girl dubiously but didn't say a word.

"Come along, Star," she said. "We can work in the spare bedroom next door." With one last nervous glance at Sam and the others, Star followed her tutor out of the room.

Eight

"**I blew it,**" Star muttered, staring down at the bowl of popcorn in front of her. She and Sam were having a snack in the presidential suite's kitchen while Mags was in the next room grading the quiz Star had just taken. "I know I totally blew it. I'll be surprised if I got more than like three questions right."

Sam reached for a handful of popcorn. "Whatever," she said, not sounding nearly as sympathetic as she usually did. "I'm sure you did fine."

Star sighed. *I can tell she's not taking this whole test thing seriously at all,* she thought gloomily. *She probably thinks it doesn't matter how I do since I'm some big superstar or whatever. But like Mrs. Nattle always says, even pop stars have to learn about stuff like Napoleon . . .*

"Star." Mags's crisp, stern voice interrupted her thoughts. "Could I speak with you, please?"

Star gulped and stood up. "Sure, Mrs. Nattle."

Leaving Sam in the kitchen, Star followed her tutor out

into the "Oval Office" room of the presidential suite. Mags was holding Star's test paper as she turned to face her.

"I won't beat around the bush, Star," Mags said. "I was very disappointed in your performance on this quiz. Here, see for yourself."

She handed over the paper. Star winced as she saw the big red D-plus at the top. "Sorry, Mrs. Nattle," she whispered, feeling horrible. "I'll do much better next time."

"Yes, you will," Mags replied. "Because starting today, we're going to be much more organized about scheduling your schoolwork into your daily agenda. I've already discussed it with Mike, and he agrees. You have a couple more hours of free time today, so I want you to spend it reading that chapter on Napoleon and then writing an essay on what you learn. I'll expect at least three pages, finished and ready for me to read by the time you leave for that radio interview this afternoon."

Star nodded miserably. She didn't blame her tutor and manager one bit for being annoyed with her performance. Ever since the tour had started, Star had been focusing less and less on her studies. That would have to change—she didn't want to disappoint her team again.

"I'll get started on that chapter right away," she said. "Just let me go tell Sam. Maybe she can stick around and help me a little—her mother is a history professor, so she knows a lot about Napoleon. Unless you don't think it's a good idea . . ."

Mags's expression softened slightly. "I suppose it would be all right if she wants to help," she said. "As long as you two stay where we can keep an eye on you."

"Thanks, Mrs. Nattle." Star smiled weakly, then turned and hurried back into the kitchen. Sam was still sitting at the small dining table, licking salt off her fingers.

"Well?" she said expectantly. "Time to shop till we drop?"

"Sorry," Star replied sadly. "I can't. I stunk all over the place on that quiz, so Mrs. Nattle wants me to do some studying now."

Sam shuddered. "I can see why you're scared of her," she said. "That tutor of yours is a total ogre!"

"No, she's totally not," Star protested. "She just really cares about education and stuff. She's always fair, but this time I let her down big-time."

Sam pushed back from the table. "I still can't believe you have to have a tutor at all," she declared. "What's the point of being a star if you still have to deal with school? Total bummer." She shrugged. "Oh well. If you're serious about this, I guess I'll take off so you can hit the books."

"Oh. Okay," Star said with a flash of disappointment. She almost mentioned her idea for Sam to help with her studying, but she held her tongue. If Sam didn't volunteer, she didn't want her to feel obligated to spend her day on someone else's schoolwork.

I mean, she hung around all this time waiting for me to take the quiz, she thought as she walked Sam to the door. *I guess I can't really blame her if she doesn't want to stick around a little longer to help me study. . . .*

"Okay, I thought this hotel gym would look like every other hotel gym in the world," Star commented. "I was all kinds of wrong."

She was standing in the American's large gym, which was located in the hotel's basement. Although most of the gym equipment was no different from anywhere else, the gym's decor was much more elaborate than the usual bright overhead lights and bare walls. The floor was painted with a huge map of the United States, and each workout station was located within the borders of a different state. The walls were adorned with a floor-to-ceiling collage depicting muscular American celebrities, from bodybuilders to movie stars to politicians.

Star was stretching out her leg muscles on a bench at the Minnesota station. She was due to leave for a dinner meeting in about an hour, and Tank had suggested a quick workout in the meantime. Star was happy to move around a little after all the studying she'd done that day.

Most of her background dancers were nearby preparing for their own workouts, while Tank stood by, overseeing their warmup. Erin and Rachel were at the bench beside Star.

"You'd better tell Tank not to run us too hard today," Rachel commented. "If he tires us out too much, we won't be able to stay up tonight."

"Tonight?" Star repeated, switching legs. "Oh, you mean the premiere party."

She had almost forgotten that the PopTV premiere was that night. After tiring out her body on the trail ride and her brain with the studying, the thought of the party made her feel downright exhausted.

"I definitely don't want to overdo it, premiere party or no premiere party," she told the twins, groaning as her leg muscles screamed in pain. "Who knew horseback riding could make someone so sore? I mean, I always thought the horse did most of the work. But I seriously doubt he's hurting as much as I am right now."

"Horseback riding?" Erin repeated. "When did you do that?"

"This morning." Star straightened up, giving her muscles a rest. "Sam took me on a trail ride at her stable."

The twins exchanged a look. "You mean that girl Samantha?" Erin asked. "The one who came backstage last night?"

"Uh-huh." Star swung her arms, loosening her shoulders. "Too bad you guys didn't have a chance to meet her. She's super cool."

Rachel took a deep breath. "Listen, Star," she said, sounding uncharacteristically serious. "We weren't sure whether to say anything. But you've become like, you know, a totally cool little sister to us or something. So you really ought to know what we heard last night."

"What my sister is trying to say," Erin said, clearly noticing Star's confused expression, "is that Samantha might not be what she seems."

"What are you talking about?" Star asked, completely perplexed. Was this another of the twins' practical jokes or something? If so, she didn't get it.

"We overheard her talking on her cell phone," Erin said. "Last night, while you were changing after the show. She stepped out of your dressing room into the hall, and I guess she didn't realize Rachel and I were just around the corner."

Rachel nodded. "We heard her bragging to someone about where she was."

"So?" Star shrugged. "That's no biggie. She was probably just excited. Most people don't spend every night hanging around backstage at a concert, you know."

"I know," Rachel said. "But then she started saying how hanging out with you was the big break she needed. And something about becoming a huge superstar herself, or something like that."

"It was a little hard to hear," Erin explained. "But it made us kind of suspicious. Anyway, we thought you should know—just in case."

"Oh. Thanks." Star lowered her head to hide her expression, pretending to adjust her shoelace. She could tell that the older girls were just trying to look out for her, and normally she would be touched that they cared enough to do that. But she didn't like what they were saying.

Okay, count them in as two more people who are down on Sam for no good reason, she thought with a flash of irritation. Then she took a deep breath and tried to be fair. *I guess it's just because they don't know her like I do. Right?*

Before she could stop it, a twinge of doubt skittered through her mind. What if they were right? After all, Star didn't retain the slightest memory of her friendship with Sam, even after spending so much time with her over the past couple of days. All she had to go by were Sam's stories about their shared past.

But that's enough, she told herself fiercely, quickly shoving her qualms aside. *Friends trust each other, and Sam is a true friend. One who already knows me a lot better than some dancers I've only known a couple of months. . . .*

Suddenly Star found herself adrift in a sudden attack of homesickness. Rachel and Erin and the others were great, but they couldn't take the place of the people she'd known and trusted forever. She realized she hadn't even e-mailed Missy since sending that short message about her riding camp news.

I really should write to her soon, she thought with yet another flash of guilt. *Maybe she remembers Sam better than I do. If so, then even Mike will have to stop doubting her. Right?*

Excusing herself from the twins, she wandered over toward Wisconsin, scuffing her feet on the painted floor. She felt guilty about doubting Samantha. After all of Sam's talk about the hours they'd spent playing together and her detailed memories of Star's parents, their kindergarten teacher, and their friends, how could she doubt her? Sam had been such a good friend to her since they'd reconnected; was this how Star repaid her? With suspicion and distrust?

"Yo, Star-baby." Tank's voice interrupted her gloomy thoughts. "Phone call for you."

Star blinked, snapping out of her reverie as Tank held out his cell phone. Star put it to her ear. "Hello?"

"Hey, Star," Sam's bubbly voice greeted her. "What's up?"

Star took a deep breath, suddenly realizing how she could make amends for her earlier thoughts. "I was just thinking I should call you," she told Sam. "What are you doing tonight?"

Nine

Sam was waiting in the Wild West suite when Star returned from her dinner meeting. As soon as she spotted Star entering, Sam flung herself across the room and almost bowled her over with a huge hug.

"I still can't believe this!" she babbled excitedly, her brown eyes shining and her whole body quivering. "I can't believe I'm going to a real live music industry big-deal premiere party! I'm ready to dance my butt off all night long!"

Star gulped. She'd been in a hurry when she'd spoken to Sam on the phone earlier, since Tank had been waiting to start the workout. Now she realized that she might not have explained well enough exactly what she was inviting the other girl to do.

"Listen, Sam," she said sheepishly. "Um, I may have given you the wrong idea about this party. It's not like a party-party—it's just supposed to look that way on TV. I mean, we'll be on satellite hookup with the PopTV studio, and there will be a party backdrop and stuff. But it'll be like two o'clock in the morning here, so once the show finishes we'll all be ready to pack it in and head home to bed."

Sam blinked, looking startled. "But it'll still mean hanging with a bunch of other celebs and glam industry insiders and eating caviar and stuff for a while in a fabulous club or somewhere, right?"

"Not really," Star admitted. "More like a bunch of paid extras and a couple of boxes of donuts in one of the hotel ballrooms."

"Oh." Sam sank down onto one of the stools at the bar. For a second she looked so crestfallen that Star thought she might burst into tears. But then she seemed to shake it off. "Well, that's okay," she said brightly. "I'm sure it will still be fun. I mean, how many regular kids even get the chance to fake-party with a pop star? I still can't believe my parents actually let me come. I'll probably have to do the dishes for the rest of my life, but I'm sure it'll totally be worth it."

Star smiled, relieved that Sam didn't seem too disappointed. "It will still be fun," she agreed. "We'll dress you up in some fabu outfit, and chances are you'll probably wind up on TV at least for a few seconds in the background. That'll be cool, right?"

"The coolest," Sam assured her. "I can't wait. It'll be way

fun just to be there for you on such a big night, you know?"

"Thanks." Star reached over and hugged her, grateful that she was being so nice about the whole situation. "Okay, we've still got hours and hours until we have to head down to the ballroom. Want to help me get ready for the party in the meantime?"

"Oh, I'm totally there!" Sam rubbed her hands together eagerly. "So what do we need to do? Should we go hit some of the designer boutiques on the Bahnhofstrasse to look for outfits to wear tonight? Oh! I have a better idea— maybe we could make some kind of cute, funny video together, like of the two of us singing 'Blast from the Past' or whatever, that they could show as part of the premiere! It'll be sort of thematic, get it? I'm like a blast from your past, so it totally works!"

Star gulped. Once again she was afraid Sam might have misunderstood what she was trying to say.

"Er, that sounds fun," she said tactfully. "But I don't think we'll have enough time for anything like that. Or even for shopping. I just meant I have a few things I need to do before the party. Like I promised to autograph a bunch of stuff that Lukas Lukas sent over—mostly props we used in the video. They're going to auction them off for charity soon, and Mike just found out that PopTV wants to show them on camera tonight. And I told Mrs. Nattle that I might as well catalog them for her while I'm at it—you know, write down exactly what we're donating and take a digital shot of each item—since I'll have to go through everything anyway to make sure I sign it all. Maybe you can help me with that?" She realized it probably wasn't exactly the kind of glamorous fun Sam was hoping for, but she gave her a hopeful smile. "That way we should get done sooner, and we'll have more time to find you something totally yummy to wear from the wardrobe boxes. Okay?"

Mike walked into the room just in time to hear the last part of Star's comments. He paused and glanced at the girls. "If y'all are making plans for the evening, make sure you include a few hours of sleep on the schedule," he said. "This premiere is going to keep you up late, and Star, you've gotta stay peppy enough to do the last few concerts before your break. Got it?"

"Got it," Star said. "We'll take a nice, long nap before the party, I swear."

As Mike moved on, Star glanced over at the other girl. Sam still looked slightly flummoxed by everything Star had just told her.

"Is this okay?" Star asked anxiously. "I hope you're not too bummed—I guess this kind of thing isn't really all that exciting."

"No, it's cool," Sam replied quickly with a smile. "It'll be tons of fun. Now come on, let's get started on that cataloging stuff. If I'm going to be possibly appearing on TV with the one and only Star Calloway, I want to make sure I have plenty of time to get myself looking fabulous!"

A couple of hours later the two girls were settling into the pair of comfortable double beds in Star's bedroom. The sun was setting outside, but the lights on the hotel building and grounds cast a bright glow through the windows at the foot of the beds.

Mags bustled into the room, checking her watch. "All right, ladies," she said, walking over and pulling down the window shades. "You'll only be able to nap for about three hours, so try not to waste any of it. I'll come back and wake you when it's time to start getting dressed for the party."

"Thanks, Mrs. Nattle," Star said, snuggling against her overstuffed pillow.

"Yes, thanks," Sam added from the other bed.

Mags smiled at them, then left the room, pulling the door

shut behind her. As soon as she was gone, Sam popped up like a jack-in-the-bed.

"This is so exciting!" she exclaimed. "I don't know how they expect us to actually sleep."

Star grinned. She was glad that Sam was still so enthusiastic even after a fairly boring evening of watching Star scribble her name all over dancing shoes and sunglasses and other props and costumes.

"You know how grown-ups are," Star said with a giggle, glancing over at the shadowy figure of Sam sitting up in her bed. "I swear, sometimes I think once you turn, like, twenty-five or thirty you're suddenly automatically obsessed with sleep. My dad's the same way—he loves his naps on Saturday afternoons!"

Sam laughed. "Really? Mine too! He always threatens to boot my behind halfway to Geneva if I wake him up."

Star giggled again, picturing Sam rolling head over heels across a big map of Switzerland. She heard Sam start giggling from the next bed.

"Wh-wh-what's so funny?" Sam demanded, still laughing.

Star laughed even harder. "I don't know," she said. "You, I guess!"

"Hey, you'd better watch what you say!" Sam said between

127

giggles. "Otherwise I'll get my dad in here to boot you to Geneva! Or maybe Paris!"

"No way!" Star clasped her stomach, which was starting to hurt from all the laughing. "I'd rather have him boot me to, like, Athens—I haven't been there yet."

By then Sam was laughing so hard she couldn't answer. Star couldn't seem to stop giggling herself. She wasn't even sure anymore what was so funny, but it felt good to let go, without worrying about cameras or reporters or what her fans might think, and laugh until she cried.

This reminds me of all the times Missy and I used to spend the night at each other's houses, she thought wistfully, her laughter fading. *Or when one of us would have a slumber party, and we and our friends stayed up all night talking and laughing and having a great time. . . .*

"Star?" Sam said. "Are you okay? You didn't actually, like, fall asleep or something, did you?"

"Nope, I'm still awake," Star said quietly. "I was just thinking how it's been a long time since I did this."

"Did what? Took a nap?"

Star shook her head, then realized Sam probably couldn't see her in the dark. "No," she said. "I mean this sort of slumber party thing. Missy and I used to hang out like this all the time. I miss that."

"I hear you," Sam said. "But hey, it's not like you're totally missing out. I mean, now you get to hang with, like, Eddie Urbane and Kynan Kane, right? Most kids would trade all the slumber parties in the world for one night of that."

"Oh, I know," Star said quickly. "I'm totally not complaining. I love my life now. But sometimes I still miss just being a regular kid, you know?"

"Sure, I guess. It must be kind of weird to have your life change so much."

Star could tell from her tone that Sam still didn't quite get it. *But it's nice that she's trying to understand where I'm coming from,* she thought, her mouth stretching into a yawn.

"Wow," she said, yawning again. "I hate to say it, but maybe we should listen to Mrs. Nattle and try to get some sleep. Because if I end up on camera tonight with big tired bags under my eyes, Mike will probably boot me right back to New Limpet."

By the time the girls finished giggling at that, they were drifting off to sleep.

"How do I look?" Sam asked breathlessly, straightening the neckline of the sparkly green top she was wearing.

Star grinned and rolled her eyes. "Fab," she said. "Just like the last forty-two times you asked."

"Sorry, guess I'm kind of nervous," Sam admitted, glancing around. It was the middle of the night, but no one would have known from looking at the large, brightly lit hotel ball-room, which was bustling with activity. "This isn't exactly an everyday kind of night for me, you know?"

Star nodded. The ballroom was decorated in a style that Lola jokingly called "ultramodern cityscape." Murals of famous American city skylines covered all four walls, and the sparse furniture looked like it came right out of a science fic-tion cartoon. Someone had hung up several large blow-up photos of Star and her album cover on the walls, and a life-size cutout of Lukas Lukas stood in the middle of the pol-ished wooden dance floor. A huge video screen set up on one wall was broadcasting PopTV. Camera and audio techs were busy testing the satellite hookup, microphone, and lights, while a small group of caterers, all of them identically dressed as the Statue of Liberty, set up a buffet at the far end of the room. Star's backup dancers were there too, clustered around the buffet table. Instead of the leotards or stage outfits they usually wore when Star saw them, they were dressed in stylish outfits that wouldn't have looked out of place in any of Europe's hottest nightclubs.

When she and Sam had arrived a few minutes earlier, Star said hello to the dancers and introduced herself to the paid extras gathered near the video screen. Several of the extras had asked for her autograph, and Sam had watched with great interest as Star obliged.

Mike strode over, a cell phone in each hand. "Think we're almost set," he said. He checked his watch. "The show should be kickin' off in about half an hour, and then we're supposed to get the nod to go on air about twenty minutes into the program."

"Sounds good," Star said. "I'll be ready."

She pushed a stray strand of curly blonde hair out of her face, being careful not to smudge the makeup Lola had applied up in the suite. Sam was still staring around in awe.

"Come on," Star told her. "I guess we have some time. We might as well pretend this is a real party, right?"

Sam grinned. "You know, for a celebrity, you make an awful lot of sense, Calloway."

For the next forty minutes Star and Sam threw themselves into enjoying the unusual party. Star was thrilled that Sam seemed to be having a great time as she watched the video cameras being set up, helped herself to the catered snacks, danced to the music on the video screen, and chattered happily with the dancers and other extras.

Finally, as the two girls were watching a video by the brand-new band VelveTeen playing on the video screen, Lola came rushing up to them. "Time for touch-ups, babydoll," she told Star breathlessly. "Hold still."

Star froze, waiting patiently as Lola quickly reapplied her lip gloss, adjusted her clothes, and fluffed up her hair. Finally the stylist stepped back, smiling with satisfaction.

"There," she said. "You look so perfect I want to put you in my pocket. But I won't." She grinned and winked, then scurried off to join the Statues of Liberty, the sound techs, and various others who were looking on from just out of range of the cameras.

"Guess that means I'm up soon," Star commented.

Sure enough, Tricia came racing up to her with Mike right behind her. "Darling, you look fabulous!" the publicist exclaimed. "So adorable! All you have to do is smile and your video is sure to be a monster hit."

"Well, maybe you'll do a little more than smile, eh?" Mike joked, winking at Star. "Just do your thing, sweetheart.

Thomas over there will point to give you your cue." He pointed to a man standing near the cameras, who gave Star a friendly little wave.

"Where should I stand?" Sam asked Mike eagerly. "Oh my gosh, I'm so nervous! This is great!"

Mike blinked and looked at her blankly. Star could tell he'd forgotten the other girl was there.

"Ah, right," he said, glancing around. "You can stand right over there with those folks, okay?"

He hooked a thumb toward the dancers and other extras, who were now gathered in the area in front of the cameras, dancing along with the music on the video screen behind them or chatting and laughing quietly in small groups. Anyone looking at them would have thought they were just a bunch of hip but regular people at a happening party.

"Okay," Sam said. "What should I do? Dance? Smile? Talk to someone? Or what?"

"Just relax, follow their lead, and pretend you're at a regular shindig," Mike told Sam kindly. "Oh, and try not to stare into the cameras, okay? I'm sure you'll do fine."

Sam gave him a thumbs-up, then hurried off to join the rest of the crowd. Star turned to face the line of huge video cameras as Mike and Tricia hurried over to stand behind them.

Star took a few deep breaths, reminding herself of what she was supposed to say. Earlier Mike had instructed her to wave and greet the worldwide TV audience, then say a few words about how much she'd enjoyed making the video. As soon as she finished, the show would cut away to the video itself. Once it finished playing, the satellite would return to Star, she would say a few more words, and that would be it.

Behind her, Star could hear the audio from the large video screen. A VJ was welcoming the audience back from a commercial break.

"And now," the VJ's voice went on, "it's time for the moment you've been waiting for—the world premiere of the latest video from Star Calloway, directed by Lukas Lukas! *In This Moment* is totally stoked to have a live video hookup with Star herself, who's taking time out from her super-successful worldwide tour to join us from way over in Zurich, Switzerland. Yo, Star, you with us?"

"Hi there, everyone!" Star cried brightly, waving to the camera as the man Mike had pointed out gave her her cue. "I'm so psyched to be able to share the premiere of my new video, 'Blast from the Past.' It was mega fun working with Lukas Lukas, and I hope you—"

"Whoo-hoo!" Suddenly a figure leaped past Star, waving both arms at the camera. "How's it going, America? Listen up, here's a preview of Star's awesome new song, okay?"

It was Sam! Star gasped in horror as the other girl started singing "Blast from the Past" at the top of her lungs.

Ten

It only took Star a split second to realize that Sam's surprise performance wasn't actually going out over the live airwaves. She could see several techs working furiously over their equipment as Mike frantically gave a finger-across-the-throat gesture to anyone who was looking. The live picture on the video screen went blank, and a second later a commercial for Zoom Juice started playing.

Meanwhile Star felt paralyzed with horror and embarrassment. What in the world had gotten into Sam? She was still singing loudly, staring intently into the main camera.

Forcing her frozen body into motion, Star leaped forward and grabbed Sam by the arm. "Hey!" she cried. "What's the deal? What are you doing?"

Out of the corner of her eye she saw Mike stalking toward them. Sam spotted him too and suddenly stopped singing, looking nervous.

"All right, young lady," Mike hissed, skidding to a stop in

front of them. His mustache was quivering with fury. "What in Sam Hill was that spectacle supposed to be? Lucky for us we were on a three-second delay and could cut away in time, or you'd really be in for it."

"What?" Sam said sullenly. "What's the big deal? I was just doing what you said—going with the moment or whatever."

Star stared at her. "Come on, Sam," she said, taking a deep breath and trying not to let her feelings of anger and betrayal take over. She wanted to hear what Sam had to say first. "What's the real story?"

"It doesn't matter," Mike growled. "I think it's time for your friend to leave. Tank can drive her home right now."

Star shook her head and grabbed his arm. "Wait, Mike, please," she begged. "I need to know why she did it." She glanced at Sam. "Well?"

For a moment Sam continued to look stubborn. Then her face crumpled into total dejection. "I'm s-sorry," she said. "I—I guess I just thought . . ."

"What?" Star prompted. She could feel Mike's anger radiating off of him, and she knew he wouldn't wait much longer before kicking Sam out. "Come on, you can say it. Whatever it is."

Sam burst into tears. "I'm sorry!" she wailed. "When I came up with this idea, it didn't seem so bad. But now that I'm in the middle of it . . ."

"Wait," Star said, a horrible thought taking hold in her mind, "are we just talking about tonight, or more than that?"

Sam bit her lip, tears running down her face and smearing the makeup Lola had carefully applied. "More than that," she said. "Way more. I made up that whole story about us knowing each other."

Star's jaw dropped, and for a second she couldn't speak. Finally she found her voice again for long enough to croak out a single word: "Why?"

"I thought hanging with you might give me a chance at becoming a star too," Sam admitted. "Plus, I figured it would be incredibly cool to tag along and, like, live your life for a while."

"But—but all that stuff you knew," Star blurted. "About New Limpet Elementary, and Missy and the gang, and my backyard, and my p-parents . . ." Her voice broke as she remembered the thoughts and feelings about her missing family she'd shared with the other girl, thinking Sam might be one of the few who could really understand.

Sam shrugged. "That's how I got the idea in the first place," she admitted, gulping back her tears. "See, my aunt's neighbor's daughter used to work at the beauty shop where your grandmother goes."

"Nans?" Star said blankly.

"Yeah," Sam said. "I guess they got to be friends, and your grandma told Margie all sorts of stuff about you, and she knew I was a fan, so—well, you get the picture." Sam had stopped crying, but she still looked miserable as she stared at Star. "I never would've done it if I knew you were so nice," she said softly. "Can you forgive me?"

Star's head was spinning so much she thought she might fall over. Instead, she turned on her heel and raced away, unable to speak to or look at Sam one second longer.

The Maxwell twins found Star a few minutes later in the women's restroom off the hotel lobby. "There you are," Erin said. "Mike sent us in to see if you were here."

Rachel nodded. "He's frantic, but not quite frantic enough to burst into the ladies' room himself." She glanced around the room, which was decorated like a Hawaiian luau.

Star wiped away a tear that was trickling down her cheek. She'd been trying hard not to cry and ruin Lola's hard work on her face. But she hadn't been totally successful.

"Sorry," she muttered. "I didn't mean to make him worry. I just had to get away for a sec."

Rachel looked sympathetic. "We heard what happened," she said. "With that girl Sam, I mean."

Star stared at herself in the palm frond–framed mirror over the sinks. "Guess you guys were right about her," she said. "Boy, do I feel like the world's biggest idiot."

"Don't say that!" Erin protested.

"Why not? It's true." Star grimaced. "I totally fell for her con job, after defending her to everyone. Just like I fell for Eddie Urbane's story when he claimed he wanted to help me find my parents. Face it—I'm just way too trusting."

Erin reached out and gave her a hug. "Hey, but that's not such a bad thing, you know," she said. "I think it's kind of cool the way you always trust people and look for the best in every situation."

"For once my sister is totally right," Rachel agreed. She grabbed a tissue from a coconut-shaped holder and used it to wipe the smeared makeup from around Star's eyes. "And if you ask me, that's a big part of what got you where you are today. I mean, lots of people have great voices and an awesome look. But that extra spark you have is what really makes you a star." She smiled. "Not to mention making you the coolest fourteen-year-old I know personally."

Star sighed loudly. "I still think life would be a lot easier if I'd stayed home in New Limpet, where people are honest."

But she couldn't help feeling a tiny bit better. The twins were right—Star's trusting nature was a big part of who she was. She couldn't stop being herself now just because she'd gotten hurt a couple of times.

"Thanks, you guys," she said, realizing how much she appreciated their friendship. They had taken a big risk in first speaking to her about Sam, and now they were still right there trying to help. "You're real friends. I guess maybe I didn't realize that until right now."

Erin shrugged. "Hey, better late than never," she joked. "Now come on—they want you back on camera after the next commercial break, and that means we've got to scoot."

Star nodded and followed them. As they left the bathroom, she saw Mike and Tank striding across the lobby, each of them holding a weeping Sam by one arm. For a moment Star almost turned away and let them go.

Then she bit her lip and stepped forward. "Hey!" she called. "Guys, wait!"

She hurried toward the trio. Sam stared at her, looking miserable. "Star, I'm so sorry!" she cried. "Please, give me a chance to explain!"

Star looked at her manager. "Do you have to kick her out now?" she asked quietly. "Maybe we should give her another chance."

Mike looked astonished. "Are you kidding?" he said. "We only have one more shot, and it's a live broadcast. We can't take any chances." He glared at Sam.

"I won't do it again," Sam said. "I swear! Star, you've got to believe me—I've learned my lesson."

Star looked at her. Sam's eyes were distressed but sincere. At least Star hoped so.

Taking a deep breath, she turned her gaze back to Mike. "I'd really prefer if we let her stay," she told him, trying to keep her lower lip from quivering. "Please. I think we should trust her."

Mike just stared back at her for a long moment. Tank kept quiet, though he dropped his hold of Sam's arm and took a step back. The only sound from their little group was Sam's sniffles.

Finally Mike sighed and rubbed his forehead. "All right,"

he said gruffly. "This prob'ly makes me dumber'n dirt, but I s'pose we can give it a whirl if you really feel that way about it, Star." He glared sternly at Sam. "But no more hijinks, young lady, or you'll have me to deal with."

"I swear," Sam promised fervently. "Star, I—"

"Later," Star interrupted her. "I want to talk to you, but right now we need to get back to the ballroom before I miss my cue."

Soon Star was back in front of the cameras. Lola was hurriedly touching up her face and hair as Mike talked to the techs. Out of the corner of her eye, Star could see Sam taking her place among the extras—and Tank and the other bodyguards moving into position nearby, just in case.

"Good luck, babydoll," Lola whispered as the director started counting down the seconds until they went live. "Knock 'em dead!"

Star smiled her thanks, then turned to face the main camera. She took a deep breath as the director counted down to one, then smiled brightly.

"Hello, PopTV!" she cried cheerfully. "I hope you liked my new video . . ."

The rest of the segment went off without a hitch. Before Star knew it, the director was calling "Clear!" and everyone was cheering.

Mike hurried out to give her a hug. "Nicely done, sweetheart," he murmured so only she could hear. "I know it wasn't easy to do that when you were so upset. You're a pro."

"Thanks, Mike," Star replied, her voice muffled by his shirt.

All around them, the "party" was already wrapping up. The caterers hurried out to clear the food away as the techs started dismantling the equipment.

Star accepted congratulations from a few more people, then turned and looked for Sam. The other girl was standing by herself near the video screen.

"Hey," Star said, hurrying toward her. "Come on. Let's talk."

Soon the two of them were huddled in a quiet corner of the room, as far as they could get from most of the activity. Sam immediately started apologizing, her words tumbling over one another as she repeated what she'd said earlier. "I just wanted to be special somehow," she finished earnestly. "You know, like, leave my mark on the world or whatever. Like you."

"I get it, I guess," Star said. Now that she was starting to understand why Sam had done what she'd done, she actually felt kind of sorry for her. "But I don't think it works that way. You need to find your own way to be special, you know?"

"What do you mean?" Sam looked uncertain.

Star shrugged. "I mean, you can make a mark on things without trying to be a singer, or hanging out with celebrities, or whatever," she said. "You've got all kinds of interests and talents and stuff of your own—you don't need to borrow mine, or anyone's."

"Talents?" Sam wrinkled her nose. "Me? I don't think so. There's nothing special about me. That's why I needed *you*."

"Come on!" Star couldn't believe the other girl could be so dense. "You're awesome! You're smart, and fun, and pretty. You speak all these foreign languages, you can ride a horse like nobody's business . . ."

"But those things aren't any big deal," Sam protested. "All kinds of ordinary people can do them."

"So what's wrong with ordinary people?" Star asked. "Lots of my favorite people in the whole world are ordinary people—my parents, Nans, Missy . . . And hey, I consider myself pretty ordinary too."

"You? Ordinary?" Sam rolled her eyes. "Yeah, right."

"Come on!" Star said sharply. "I thought you'd gotten to know me a little these past few days. So tell me, am I some kind of freak? An alien from outer space?"

Sam lifted one shoulder in a half shrug. "No."

"Then why did you think you could use me like that?" Star bit her lip. "I thought we were friends. You really hurt my feelings, you know."

Sam gulped loudly. "I know," she said. "I guess I wasn't thinking about that at the time. I mean, at first I hardly even thought of you as a real person. You were Star Calloway, you know? But then we started to hang out, and I really liked you, and I wasn't sure what to do. I wanted to tell you the truth, but I figured you'd kick me to the curb."

Star smiled ruefully. "Hey, it almost happened," she said. "Mike and Tank weren't kidding about tossing you."

"I know," Sam said. "Thanks for stopping them. Anyway, I hope you can forgive me, but I don't blame you if you're sick of me and never want to see me again. Either way, I just want you to know that I'll always think of you as a true friend—whether you become the hugest superstar ever to live, or decide to quit the tour and move back to New Limpet tomorrow."

Star took a deep breath as she thought back over all their

conversations. How much of them had been sincere? She might never know. Could she live with that, and stay friends with Sam anyway?

"By the way," Sam added, breaking into her thoughts. "I also wanted to tell you, I really do think you should record that 'Star Bright' song. I meant every word I said about that—I wasn't just trying to butter you up or anything."

Star smiled. "Thanks," she said, her worries melting away. Who cared about what had happened in the past? What mattered was that they both wanted to move forward and start over. "Oh, and by the way—apology accepted."

Sam blinked. "Really?" she exclaimed, her eyes brightening. "Whoo-hoo!"

Her whoop was so loud that several of the adults glanced over at them from across the room. But Star hardly noticed. She laughed out loud at the other girl's delight, then braced herself as Sam flung herself toward her for a hug.

Less than an hour later Sam was on her way home in the limo while Star sat on her bed upstairs in the Wild West suite. It was very late, and she was tired despite her nap. But before she went to sleep, she pulled out her computer. She and Sam had promised to keep in touch, and Star wanted to make sure she entered her new friend's e-mail address and IM name before she lost the scrap of paper Sam had scribbled them on.

She quickly took care of that, then clicked open a new e-mail document. There was just one more thing she wanted to take care of before she went to sleep.

From: singingstar01

To: MissTaka

Subject: Catching up

Hi Missy,

Sorry it took me so long 2 write back 2 U about the horse camp thing. The last few days were kinda busy—remind me 2 tell U when I C U about this girl I met here in Switzerland named Sam. I think u'd like her.

NEway, I just wanted 2 tell u how awesome it is that ur parents r letting u ride this summer. U r so lucky—but u totally deserve it! I know u'll have a gr8 time, and I want 2 hear all about it, OK? That way it'll b almost like we R doing it 2gether.

Can't wait 2 C U when I come home next week!

Hugs 'n kisses,

Yr bff,

Star

Catch Star's next act

#6 *Someday, Some Way*

Star has been keeping so busy on her European tour that she hasn't had much time to get homesick. Then, during a brief break in her schedule, she flies home for her grandmother's birthday, she realizes all that she's missing back home: hanging out with her friends, new stores in town, Missy's new haircut, and more.

Is all the sacrifice worth it? Will Star decide to give up the life of a rock goddess to return to her roots as an ordinary small-town girl?

Find out in *Someday, Some Way*, the next book in the Star Power series!

star power

by ★ Catherin Hapka

She's beautiful, she's talented, she's famous.

She's a star!

Things would be perfect
if only her family
was around to help
her celebrate. . . .

Follow the
adventures of
fourteen-year-old
pop star
Star Calloway

★ **A new series from Aladdin Paperbacks!**

some day some way